# THE ROYAL GROOM

*Wrong Way Weddings Book 4*

## LORI WILDE &
## PAM ANDREWS HANSON

**M**y other car is a limo.

Leigh Bailey returned the heavy gas pump hose and glimpsed the bumper sticker on her shabby little convertible. Rain blew in her face, obscuring her vision for a moment and taking away her breath.

Her chances of ever owning a limo on her salary were nil, but wouldn't it be nice to sit in a spacious back seat while a chauffeur braved the Florida storm to tank up for her?

Never mind that she shared the same last name as her wealthy cousins, *the* billionaire Baileys from Detroit. Her branch of the family was church mouse poor.

Well, a girl could dream, couldn't she? Meanwhile, she had a long trip ahead of her. She sprinted toward the convenience store, unsuccessfully dodging puddles.

The rain tried to follow her into the small building, adding to the water on the floor before she could shut the door. For a storm that was supposed to bypass Florida, Hurricane Jeff was delivering a deluge.

She stood for a moment, letting water run off her red nylon rain poncho, and brushed away the drops streaming down her forehead. Her car was less than twenty feet away at the pump, but she'd still gotten soaked.

In a hurry to be on her way before the storm worsened, she got in line behind a tall dark-haired man in a green jacket. By the time she located the right credit card in her oversized canvas shoulder bag, she realized he was reading, not paying for gas.

In fact, he was literally studying the front page of the *Insider,* one of the country's sleaziest tabloids.

"Excuse me," she said, stepping around him and catching a glimpse of his long, lean jaw and strong features— hardly the kind of profile she'd expect to see buried in a gossip rag.

He gave a small start and hastily shoved the copy of the *Insider* back on the rack, as though she'd caught him doing something dirty. Without meeting her gaze, he hurried over to the beverage case.

There was something unusual about the way he

moved—a grace that was hard to define. She'd never seen anyone who looked less like a tabloid junkie, even though she hadn't had a good look at his face.

"The power of the fake news," she muttered under her breath, annoyed by her own curiosity. What was so interesting in the *Insider*?

She ignored the bored-looking boy waiting to take her card and quickly scanned the tabloid headlines. She didn't think it was the story on aliens landing in Ohio that had him so intrigued. It had to be the other page-one story: ***Soap Heiress Dumps Prince Max for Bullfighter.***

*Darcy Wolridge shocked friends and family by eloping with the idol of the Spanish bullring, Jose Perez, amidst rumors she was number one on Prince Max's list of prospective brides.*

*The brokenhearted Maximilian of Schwanstein is believed to be in the U.S. shopping for a bride. Who will be the lucky lady now that lovely Darcy has shattered his hopes?*

A huge grainy picture showed the heiress draped on the shoulder of a macho-looking guy in a snakeskin jacket. The article continued on page eleven, but Leigh had seen enough. Darcy and the prince had been an item for weeks in the fairy-tale world of the tabloids. Leigh didn't want to read some sappy fiction about Maximilian's broken heart.

*Her* article about the prince would be classy—if she could find him. And if he'd talk to her.

Her credentials from *Celebrity* magazine carried more weight than an *Insider* reporter's, but only because she worked for the hippest gossip magazine around. A magazine that served up content in print, online, and TV. Both magazines chased the rich, the famous, and the ridiculous, but Prince Max could change all that for her.

If she could convince him to give her a serious, insightful interview, it might be her ticket to a better job. She'd have a good chance at moving to *Issues*, owned by the same media conglomerate as *Celebrity,* but a world away in content. Their writers didn't ride in limos, either, but neither did they have to write about rock stars in rehab and supermodels' skin secrets.

First, she had to find the prince. All she had to go on was a tip from her uncle Paul Donovan in West Palm Beach. An avid stamp collector, he'd picked up a rumor on the internet that the prince might pay a visit to the president of the Schwanstein Stamp Collectors Society. Max would supposedly stay at a plush Paradise Beach hotel, and that was Leigh's destination. Her editor thought the lead was solid enough to authorize travel expenses.

Leigh hurried back to her car, trying to believe

the weather report she'd heard just before leaving Miami, where she worked out of *Celebrity*'s East Coast office. But if this was only a rain squall, she was Lady Gaga.

Torrential rain, driven by the wind, blanketed the windshield and swept across the on-ramp with the force of a giant fire hose as she crept back onto the highway. She wanted to wait out the storm in some nice dry place, but the prince was notorious for keeping on the move.

"If you'll tell your real story to a sympathetic reporter," she said, rehearsing her appeal, "it might stifle some of the silly rumors."

She had a more immediate problem: the taillights ahead of her had vanished in a wall of water. She dropped her speed to a crawl, wondering whether it was worse to hit the car ahead or be rear-ended because she was going too slow.

Traffic was coming to a stop. Flashing red lights were visible through the downpour, and she realized cars were leaving the highway. A policeman in a tent-like slicker was waving everyone off to the right.

Never one to docilely obey, she rolled down her window far enough to shout at the cop.

"What's wrong, Officer?"

"Highway's flooded. Keep moving, please." He

made an impatient gesture and looked as if he wanted to give her car a kick to get it going.

She complied. She was an intrepid reporter, not a fool.

Her sense of direction was about as reliable as the weather, so she followed the taillights ahead of her, hoping the driver knew an alternate route north. *She* certainly didn't, and she had no cell service for her GPS.

The cars gradually thinned out, making her wonder where all the highway traffic had gone. Apparently, this was an old state highway, neglected after the interstate was built. No traffic was visible in the oncoming lane, but she felt safer moving slowly through the downpour, not having to worry about passing.

Suddenly a great black shape streaked past her on the left, throwing up a ton of water. Her small car rocked sideways, and Leigh's heart did crazy flip-flops. She saw the aggressively bright taillights of the dark sedan as it cut in front of her, then her right front wheel skidded off the pavement onto the rain-softened dirt shoulder.

"What the devil!" Max saw the car he'd passed slide

off the pavement, and for an instant, he was afraid it would roll.

He brought the rented sedan to a stop and flipped on the hazard lights, unwilling to risk pulling onto the narrow shoulder. Dashing out into the rain, he was relieved to see the driver hadn't lost control. The axle of the little convertible had sunk in muck, but it was a mishap, not a tragedy. Still, he couldn't just leave the driver there alone.

Damn!

He'd pulled too close to the car's rear trying to read the bumper sticker, then been forced to pass because the convertible was moving slower than any car should on a highway.

The real blame should go to the American habit of putting signs on their bumpers. The single sentence on the back of this jalopy was ludicrous: *My other car is a limo.*

He wouldn't forget that one in a hurry; it had resulted in one more glitch in his plans. What else could go wrong on this trip? Darcy's defection still rankled. She'd promised not to let him down this time, but his distant American cousin hadn't changed since she'd thrown sand in his face when they were toddlers playing on the beach.

His American mother's cousin was always too busy playing to pay attention to her daughter—unlike his own parents, who'd been stern but loving. He still missed his mother, who'd died seven years ago in a car accident when he was twenty-five.

Sometimes, though, he wished his father would remarry, instead of worrying so much about his son's single status.

He reached the convertible and opened his mouth to offer assistance, but he didn't have a chance to speak.

"You ran me off the road. Look at this!" The driver got out in the rain and gestured furiously at her tires, so mired in mud it was obviously futile to try driving the vehicle out.

He knew a calm reasonable response was his best defense, but all he could do was stare at the red-caped woman who was soundly berating him.

He'd never seen such a beautiful face.

Her hair was pulled back in a ponytail and plastered to her head by the rain, but she didn't need salon-perfect hair to give an illusion of beauty.

She possessed the real thing: exquisite bone structure, dramatically slashed brows, and a perfect nose, straight and a trifle larger than the pert little knobs Americans seemed to prefer, but very much to his liking.

When she stepped closer to continue venting anger—and perhaps fear at the close call—he looked into a unique shade of hazel eyes set off by long dark lashes. Her lips were full, especially the bottom one, suggesting a mouth made to give pleasure.

It was a shame she was also brash and rude, common enough faults in American women but highly regrettable in such a sensual creature.

"It's too bad you weren't driving your other car," he said mildly.

"What?"

"Your limo."

"You were close enough to read my bumper sticker through the rain?"

"I enjoy a good joke," he said, not wanting her to think he was too naive to appreciate the humor of it. He surprised himself by caring about her opinion of him. "What can I do to assist you?"

"Push my car out of the mud."

He walked the length of the vehicle, pretending to consider the possibility, but of course there was none.

"I'm afraid you'll need a tow truck."

"Does your phone have service?" she asked, frantically pressing the screen of her device.

Max checked his. No luck. "No, I don't. I'll be happy to drive you to a phone."

"Oh, great. I can stay here and watch my car sink in muck or go off with a total stranger."

She sounded so dejected he was ready to forgive her for distracting him with a bumper sticker—but not for calling him an idiot.

"Allow me to introduce myself. I'm Max Frederick." He offered her a wet hand—Americans liked their palm-to-palm ritual.

She only stared, and Max had seen that expression of recognition before—too many times. He should have given her another name, instead of the one he used when he traveled.

"Max for Maximilian?" she asked suspiciously.

He barely nodded, mesmerized by the way she ignored the rain pelting her face and head. He couldn't think of any woman of his acquaintance who would stand in a downpour without worrying about how she looked.

Did this one realize she was a ravishing beauty in any circumstances, or was she free of vanity? The answer seemed important, but this wasn't the time or place to explore it.

The prince.

It made sense, but still, she was stunned. "Maximilian Augustus Frederick of the Principality of Schwanstein?"

"If I were this prince," he said in lightly accented English, "would you get into my car and end this ridiculous conversation in the rain?"

"I don't have much choice, no matter who you are."

"Come on, before my car gets hit. I didn't dare pull off the highway."

Dumbfounded at recognizing him, Leigh didn't resist when he grabbed her hand and started pulling her toward his lights. She had to half run to match his long-legged stride, but she wasn't going to let him drag her.

Prince Max!

He'd run her off the road—sort of—just because he was curious about her bumper sticker. Now he was going to rescue her—in a manner of speaking.

"Wait! I need my purse!"

She jerked her hand away from his, surprised at how his palm had been warming her, and ran back toward her car. Half afraid he'd abandon her, she grabbed the shoulder bag and her duffel, knowing this was no time to be without her tape recorder. Then, more by habit than conscious thought, she locked the car door and raced back to the prince.

Even in this blinding storm, he opened the door for her. Her teeth were chattering so hard she could hardly mutter a thank-you.

"Do you have a chill?" he asked solicitously as he slid behind the wheel.

"No, my teeth always chatter after a narrow escape from death."

How rude, she thought as soon as the words were out of her mouth. Oh well, it was better than having him suspect how excited she was to be in the same car with him. Forget limos! She was with the prince.

She'd interviewed hundreds of famous people since coming to *Celebrity* magazine five long years ago, but this opportunity was special. She told herself it was only because he could give her career a tremendous boost, but pictures didn't do him justice. He was gorgeous—even if he didn't have enough sense not to tailgate just to read a bumper sticker.

"Help me watch for a place to stop," he said. "The storm's getting worse."

"Hurricane Jeff is supposed to miss Florida."

"Now all the little boys named Jeff will have a new nickname—Hurricane Jeff."

"It doesn't seem fair, does it?" She clenched her jaws to stop the chattering, appreciating the small talk. It gave her time to regain her composure. "They're such nasty storms; they should have names no one would ever give their children—Hurricane Dracula, Hurricane Frankenstein..."

His laugh came from deep inside his chest, and

his good humor didn't seem contrived. "Let me see, do we have any female monsters? There was Medusa."

She wanted to keep the game going, but her mind was too full of the man beside her to come up with any diabolical females.

"How did you recognize me?" he asked, abruptly switching from the safe subject of naming hurricanes. "I had a full beard until recently."

She hesitated a moment to weigh her options and decided it was a bad idea to try to deceive him. After all, she didn't work for a rag like the *Insider*. Not quite.

"I've done a little research. You were clean-shaven until three or four years ago."

"How odd you should know that." His voice lost some of its warmth, and his accent seemed more pronounced.

"The truth is, Prince— What should I call you? Your Highness?"

"You can call me Max, unless you're one of that infernal breed who call themselves reporters."

"Your Highness," she said, struggling for a way to win him over without actually licking his boots.

"I take it that a reporter's exactly what you are. My luck on this trip," he said woodenly, "has been incredibly bad."

"I don't work for a sleazy tabloid like the one you

were reading at the gas station," she said. "*Celebrity* magazine is a monthly, and what I hope to do is a really insightful piece about you, something to quiet all the rumors."

"What you hope to do isn't what you're going to do," he said. "As soon as I find a safe place to leave you, our brief acquaintanceship is over."

"You're above talking to a legitimate magazine writer, but you didn't seem to have any scruples about reading the *Insider*—without even buying it." She knew it was self-defeating to antagonize him, but he had no right to look down his nose at her profession.

"It's not a habit of mine, I assure you. I had a very good reason this time."

"No doubt you did. Some people love to see their names in print, and we both know you made headlines in the *Insider*—again."

"You couldn't be more mistaken, but then, I've never met a reporter who didn't excel at leaping to conclusions. Are you watching for a phone booth? Do they even have those anymore? Never mind, I see some sort of motel up ahead. I'll stop there."

"Why were you so interested in the *Insider*?" she persisted. "And why lump all reporters together?"

"I didn't choose to satisfy your curiosity the first time you asked, so why persist? That, Miss..."

"Leigh. Leigh Bailey. If you're going to insult me, at least acknowledge I'm a person with a name."

"Miss Bailey, do you have any idea how much grief your profession causes? I can't live a normal life because paparazzi hound me and reporters harass me."

"There's nothing normal about the life of a prince."

"No, there isn't," he said wearily, pulling off the road and stopping beside a squat little building with bright-pink siding.

"The Pink Flamingo—cottages to rent by day or week," she read from a dingy sign featuring a rust-streaked fuchsia bird.

Farther down the gravel drive was a scattering of squat little bungalows that looked too small to contain a double bed. They had the same garish siding, probably a 1950's renovation.

"Shall I come inside to make sure you can get a tow?" Max asked.

She wanted to suggest a more appropriate place for him to go, but as long as there was a slight chance of an interview, she'd watch what she said.

Would her editor go along with an article on how the prince ran her off the road trying to read her bumper sticker, then refused to be interviewed?

Doubtful. Unlike the *Insider*, her magazine liked to include a few hard facts about the subject.

The office was deserted.

Max impatiently pressed a metal bell sitting on the counter, but Leigh didn't know how he could summon anyone in a one-room shack. She did spot an antiquated black dial phone on a small desk against the far wall.

"I'll see if I can find a tow truck," she said, invading the proprietor's side of the counter.

"Perhaps you should ask permission to use the phone," Max suggested.

"I'm only going to make a quick call."

"Not on that phone you ain't, missy." A wizened old man in a yellow slicker and rain hat tramped into the office through the door they'd used, startling her so much she jumped.

Leigh heard a soft chuckle from Max.

"I'll be glad to pay," she said. "All I want to do is call a tow truck. My car was forced off the road, and it's stuck in the mud."

"Don't you people listen to the radio? We're under a hurricane warning. No one's going to go after your car now."

"Hurricane Jeff was supposed to miss Florida," she said.

"Yup, but no one bothered to tell the hurricane."

"It wouldn't hurt to call a service station," Max said. "I may be able to offer some inducement."

"Only way you can call anybody is to go outside and holler. Phone's dead. Power's off, too. If you two got a place to go near here, you'd better get there quick."

"We don't." Max answered for both of them. "We'll have to ride it out in the car."

"Bad idea, Mister. Lotta wires down in town. Main Street's flooded. Took me forty minutes to get back here, and it's only a couple miles. Had to detour around a toppled tree down the road a piece."

"Then do you suggest we rent two of your cottages?" Max asked skeptically.

"Could if I had 'em. Got only one left. Two hundred bucks a night, take it or leave it."

"We'll leave it. Your rates are right here." Leigh tapped her finger on a grimy square of cardboard taped to the counter. "Thirty-three dollars a night, but we won't be staying over. We just need a place this afternoon to weather the storm."

"That's the off-season rate. Hurricane rate's two hundred."

"We'll take it." Max took out his wallet and slapped a credit card on the counter.

"No plastic. Cash only."

The old man's Adam's apple bobbed in his skinny

neck, and Leigh could see he was enjoying his moment of power.

"This is a platinum card," Max argued. "It's good anywhere in the world."

"Not in Lavern, Florida, it ain't. But I'll forget the tax, seein' as how the telly-vision ain't workin'."

"Big of you." Max was rummaging in his wallet, sorting out bills—foreign bills. "Here's twenty, forty. Yes, and some ones. Forty-three dollars. That's all I have, and it's more than your usual rate."

"Too bad." The old man clicked his dentures. "Too bad for you, not me. With that fancy interstate closed, folks are flocking this way. I'll fill 'er up, no problem."

"Let me see what I have," Leigh reluctantly offered, hating to meet the old crook's price.

She'd cashed her paycheck just before leaving Miami, and like any good reporter, she carried enough cash for emergencies. The prince watched, tight-lipped and scowling, as she made up the difference from her billfold.

"Are you embarrassed because a woman is paying?" she asked Max under her breath, enjoying the upper hand for a brief moment.

"Of course not."

His gaze met hers, the whites of his eyes an arresting contrast to his deep-brown pupils, and she felt tingly all over. She was cold from the rain, but his gaze was definitely warming her. Dark brows set close to his eyes made them even more dazzling, and she had to look away first or risk being vaporized by his penetrating stare.

The old man recounted the cash, then made it disappear inside the rubbery depths of his slicker.

"Number seven—lucky number," he said, banging a key attached to a large chunk of wood on the counter. "No one ever walks away with one of these babies in his pocket. That'll be two dollars key deposit, refundable when you turn it in."

"That's outrageous," the prince protested. "You've already robbed us."

"Here's your two dollars." Leigh was thinking of an exposé to get even. She'd title it: *Highway Robbery on Florida's byways.*

"You folks want to rent a lantern? Power's off."

"For two hundred dollars you don't even supply light?" It was her turn to be indignant.

"Kerosene lantern. Don't suppose you two ever used one, but any fool can figure it out." He took one from the floor behind the counter. "Raise the wick with this here knob and light it—I'll throw in a box of wooden matches—then put the globe back on."

"How much?" Max asked resignedly.

"Just three bucks—gotta cover the cost of kerosene and maintenance."

Leigh counted out her change to pay him.

"Checkout time is noon. If you want to stay another day, let me know then."

Max made a low sound in his throat that intimidated Leigh but not the jolly innkeeper. Of course, he didn't know he was dealing with royalty.

"We'll only be here a few hours," she said with more confidence than she felt.

Meanwhile, it occurred to her the prince couldn't possibly be too mean-spirited to grant her an interview after she'd paid for most of the room.

## ❧ 2 ❧

"I admit I shouldn't have pulled so close to read your bumper sticker," Max said. "But you were barely moving. I'll reimburse you for the room and your car, but don't think of this as an opportunity to blackmail me into an interview. I don't pay my debts by baring my soul."

She made a chuffing noise.

He looked around the small room with distaste. It was the first time he'd ever been in a room with paneled walls and a ceiling to match.

The knotty pine had a thick yellow varnish, and the narrow windows admitted a minimum of light. He put the lantern on a scarred dresser and wondered if it wouldn't be better to leave the woman here and take his chances in the car.

"That's not what I'm suggesting," she said,

sounding a little miffed. "I just thought, since we're both stranded here, we might...chat."

"And will you swear no word of our conversation will ever appear in print?" he challenged, surprised to realize he enjoyed verbally sparring with the attractive reporter.

"Maybe we should just play a game to pass the time—say twenty questions?" she asked hopefully, still holding her duffel bag in one hand and her purse in the other, perhaps at a loss where to put them.

"There's room for your bag here," he said, taking the duffel and moving the lantern to one side. "Shall I light this?"

"I guess it's better than sitting in the gloom. I've never heard the wind so loud." She glanced around as though doubting that the walls were strong enough to withstand hurricane-force gales.

"We're probably far enough inland to escape the worst of it." He wanted to be reassuring, but he didn't know what to expect from his first hurricane.

"I'm going to see if towels come with the room. I'd love to dry off." She unsnapped her dripping red poncho and hung it on a narrow metal rack using one of three wire hangers.

He'd wondered if her figure would be as eye-catching as her face. It was. A sleeveless brown top clung to full breasts and trim waist.

She wore a small gold locket around her neck, and he wondered if it held her boyfriend's picture. A woman this beautiful surely must have a man in her life. The thought sparked a totally irrational surge of envy.

When she turned toward the bathroom, he couldn't help admiring her slender shapely legs. She was wearing short shorts, and her backside was nicely rounded. Her skin was honey tan and as smooth as polished ivory, and he caught his breath at the impact she had on him.

She reached for the knob of the closed door, and he noticed how graceful her arms were. Her wrists were delicate, the left encircled by a narrow gold watchband.

"I'll be a few minutes," she said. "My hair is soaked."

"No doubt we'll be here a while," he said. "The storm seems to be getting worse."

"We're blessed with towels," she said, poking her head through the doorway. "Would you like one?"

She dangled it from one pink-nailed hand.

"Very much, thank you."

He walked the few steps necessary to take it from her, wondering what color her hair would be when it was dry. In fact, he was eager to see it hanging long and silky to her shoulders. When she closed the door, he hoped she'd hurry back.

What was he thinking? Of all the women on the face of the earth, a reporter was the one he absolutely shouldn't seduce. His first criterion in a woman was discretion; he shuddered thinking of the kind of kiss-and-tell article she might write.

If he'd stuck to his itinerary, he wouldn't be in this fix. He was familiar enough with the U.S. to expect the unexpected whenever he visited, which was fairly often. He'd been coming here since childhood because his mother had been an American.

His parents' courtship had been the stuff of fairy tales: a handsome young prince falling madly in love with a commoner.

He shivered and realized he was in a deplorable state, wet enough to wring a gallon of rainwater from his clothing. His jacket had not lived up to its water-repellent label. Below his waist he was soaked to the skin, his trousers clammy on his legs.

His clothes were at the hotel in Paradise Beach, perhaps being brushed and pressed by his valet at this very moment. He should have gone straight to meet the stamp collectors.

It was sheer bad luck that his decision to drive alone on a side trip to see an old acquaintance—a model on a shoot—had resulted in an auto mishap.

With a reporter, no less. She was probably the only person between the airport and his destination who'd have recognized him.

He couldn't change the situation now, although he would gladly have hired a limo to take her off his hands. But he was stuck, so he might as well take off his pants and try to get dry. With a wary glance at the closed door, he started undressing.

The bathroom was cramped and dingy—in fact, it was only a cubicle with a shower—but Leigh was in no hurry to leave it.

No, that wasn't true. She was *dying* to get back to the prince. She just needed to think of a way to wear down his resistance. How could she convince him to give her an interview? He was as evasive as he was sure of himself.

He also had a face to inspire dreams. All his features were totally in harmony: the long sweep of his lightly shadowed jaw, the slight cleft in his chin, and those full pouty lips. She shivered and tried to blame it on being chilled, scrubbing at her arms with a dry towel to warm up.

She should have her head examined for even thinking of the prince as a hunk. She'd been proposi-

LORI WILDE & & PAM ANDREWS HANSON

tioned by rock musicians and pinched by their managers, but never ever had she responded to a come-on from a man she wanted to interview.

Prince Max wouldn't get past her guard—though it annoyed her that he wasn't likely to try. She wasn't in the same league as supermodels and heiresses.

Was there any chance he'd do what princes in fairy tales did: grant her one wish? Or maybe that was genies and fairy godmothers who did that. Still, there had to be a way to get her story.

Without her brush, which was packed away in her clothes in the trunk of the car, there wasn't much more she could do with her hair. She let it hang loose in a tangled cascade.

Just as she was leaving the bathroom, the whole cottage shuddered under the impact of the wind. Some shelter! The big bad wolf could blow this place down without even exerting himself.

She stepped into the bedroom. And laughed out loud.

She hadn't seen a costume this silly since Greek week at the university.

"Are you trying to look like Julius Caesar?"

"Please, at least let me be Mark Anthony." Max grinned and did a security check on the tuck holding up his toga, a sheet stripped from the now-rumpled double bed.

She couldn't stop giggling.

"Am I that ridiculous?" he asked.

"No, you look like you were born to the sheet —toga."

"My trousers are soaked. I'll hang them over the shower rod, if you don't mind."

He quickly made a bundle of them, but not before she got a glimpse of a silky black triangle. No jockey shorts or shapeless boxers for this prince! They were the sexiest men's briefs she'd ever seen outside of a men's store.

"They'll never dry in the bathroom. It's too damp. Hang them over the chair and move it closer to the lantern."

"That wouldn't be appropriate."

"I grew up with an older brother. I've seen men's underwear."

He gave her a withering look and hung his pants on the chair, but not before he stuffed the briefs into one of the pockets.

He wasn't disappointed about her hair. It had dried to a lustrous dark-golden blond.

She slipped out of her sandals and propped one of the two pillows against the headboard of the bed.

With the ease of a cat curling up on its cushion, she sat and leaned against it, crooking her legs and hugging her knees.

"Will you at least answer one question for me—off the record?" she asked.

"Will you promise not to repeat it in your magazine?"

"Yes, I promise I won't write about it."

He eyed her skeptically. "Is your word any more reliable than the claim on your bumper sticker?"

"Yes, I keep my word." She didn't sound happy about it.

"Very well, ask."

"Why were you reading the *Insider*?"

He took a deep breath, deciding how much to reveal. She smiled encouragingly, hunching her shoulders in a way that made him imagine putting his arm around them.

"I'm concerned about one of the people in the article," he said.

"You really were hoping to marry Darcy Wolridge?"

To her credit, she sounded genuinely astonished. It was good to know not everyone swallowed a story like that.

"Not exactly."

He walked over to stare out one of the two rain-fogged windows, feeling ridiculous but considerably drier in his makeshift wrappings.

This reporter was beautiful by any man's standards, and he thought his were high. So many women were thrust into his path that he sometimes felt like a breeding stud being led to the mares. This visit in the States was going to be especially bad, thanks to the press. He was still seething over another tabloid's story that had linked him to a thrice-married actress.

When he married—and he'd get around to it in his own good time—it would be to a woman who had the qualities he respected: honesty, loyalty, dignity, and strength of character. Beauty would be only an added bonus, but not one in short supply in his circle. How could he make a reporter understand his feelings?

He decided not to try.

"Even if I were inclined to marry my own cousin, I'd hesitate to form a union with Darcy. We know each other's weaknesses too well."

"She's your cousin?"

He couldn't hold back a grin of triumph. "If you'd researched thoroughly..."

"I didn't have time to be thorough." She slid off the bed and glared at him. "My uncle Paul saw on the internet you were going to Paradise Beach."

"How on earth...?"

"The stamp collector connection. Isn't one of your stops a visit to the president of the Schwanstein Stamp Collectors Society in Paradise Beach?" It was her turn to grin.

"It's on my itinerary. Selling stamps to collectors is a significant source of revenue in my country."

"Let's get back to Darcy."

"She's actually my mother's cousin's daughter," he said, wondering why he had an uncharacteristic urge to explain things to her. "We played together on holidays when we were children. Since I don't have any siblings, I look on her as an errant little sister."

"Then you don't approve of the bullfighter?"

He shrugged. "It won't last. It's only a matter of how much of her fortune he'll be able to appropriate."

"That's a cold-blooded assessment. Maybe they really love each other."

"Do you believe marriages are sure to be happy if the bride and groom are besotted with each other?"

"No, I guess not. It didn't work out that way with my parents." A loud noise made her jump. "What was that?"

"Something hit the cottage. I'll take a look." He flung open the door with predictable results. The small overhang wasn't enough to keep rain from gusting through the opening.

"Hey, don't go out there! It was probably only a branch!" She grabbed his arm and attempted to pull him back.

"You're probably right." He had to push hard to close the door again. "The wind isn't strong enough to flatten this place, or the owner would have boarded up the windows." He wasn't entirely convinced, but it certainly sounded good.

"You're damp again," she said.

He was more than damp. Rain had pelted his bedsheet toga, soaking the front so thoroughly she could see dark shadows and unmistakable contours under the flimsy covering.

"So I am." He looked down, then backed toward the bed.

His hair, dried to an unruly mass of dark-brown curls before he opened the door, was wetly black again, and she'd seen an outline of the royal anatomy that made the room seem as hot as a sauna.

"If you'll kindly turn your back a moment..." he said.

"Sure."

This couldn't be happening. If she wrote about it,

even the most gullible reader would think she'd made it up.

"You can turn around now."

He'd discarded the sheet and wrapped himself in a fuzzy yellow blanket stripped from the bed, securing it under his arms so his shoulders were bare.

And what magnificent shoulders they were.

Nicer than any she could invent in a fantasy: bronzed from the sun with a light sprinkling of freckles and so sleekly muscled his flesh seemed carved from the finest marble. She looked away; she had to. The urge to stroke them with her fingertips was almost overwhelming.

He walked around the end of the bed and stopped a few steps from her.

"You look like a big chicken," she teased, focusing on the part of him that was securely covered.

"You could at least have said rooster." He moved away from the lantern into the shadows, apparently not pleased to have his dignity called into question.

She studied him.

"Why do you enjoy being a reporter?" he asked, startling her a bit. Had he suddenly realized she was a potentially interesting person?

"I love talking to people. The world sees the famous in terms of what they've accomplished. Sometimes I find surprisingly nice human beings behind the facades."

"And sometimes not?"

"I could tell you about a folksy guitarist who made me watch his pet boa gulp down a poor little mouse—"

Suddenly there was a tremendous crash, one that made the floor shake.

She froze, unsure whether to run or crawl under the bed.

"What was that?" she gasped, her astonishment doubled when Max rushed over and put his arms around her.

Something ominous had happened out there. She did the natural thing: she hugged him back.

"You'll be alright. Probably a tree," he said in a low comforting voice, cradling her cheek against the fuzzy blanket.

How could she let him hold her like this? What kind of signal was she sending? He might even think the F-word: faking! Women probably played the damsel in distress for his benefit all the time.

"I'll be fine." She pulled away with the greatest reluctance. "You probably think I'm a sissy."

"No." He chuckled softly. "But if you're trying to make me feel brave and protective, you've succeeded admirably."

Before she could decide how to take that, the door blew open, slamming against the wall and letting the storm invade their precarious sanctuary.

He reacted instantly, getting behind it and forcing it shut with his shoulder.

"I thought I locked it."

"You did." She hung back.

"This time I'll use the chain, but I can't guarantee it'll hold."

"Prop the chair against it, too." She tossed his trousers on the bed and carried the wooden-backed chair to the door.

"Can't hurt," he said, following her advice.

Leigh shuddered, wondering if the storm would ever pass. It was hard to believe they were only on the fringe of Hurricane Jeff.

"There's one more thing we can do," he said. He padded gingerly across the wet, faded blue carpet on bare feet.

"Get under the bed?" She tried not to think of what could happen on top of the bed.

"Close. I think the safest corner is over there. Help me move the mattress."

"Our own little fortress?"

"Something like that."

She helped him make a nest, spreading the remaining sheet and tossing down the two pillows. As an afterthought, she grabbed her duffel before huddling down in the corner behind the mattress.

"Can you think of anything else?" he asked before lowering himself beside her, still trailing the blanket.

She could think of several things, all of them involving more hugging. She could feel one of his long muscular legs against her calf, tickling her, creating its own kind of electricity. She remembered that the blanket was all he was wearing.

"You don't need a change of clothes now," he said, bumping against her duffel, "although I wish I could say the same thing."

"My clothes are still in the car. This is just my travel bag."

She dug into the bag, unintentionally letting him see her camera and tape recorder.

"I hope you don't have any ideas about taking my picture." He reached over and restrained both her hands with his.

She should have resented the gesture, but his fingers were more caressing than invasive. Imagine, a prince with hard, strong hands.

"I was going to share my emergency rations with you. There's not much, but I didn't expect to be stranded in a hurricane."

He watched her suspiciously, his dark eyes following her every move as she handed him a can of soda and a plastic bag of trail mix. He didn't relax until she zipped up the duffel and pushed it aside.

They sipped and nibbled, and she tried to watch him in the dim light without seeming to stare. She caught a faint whiff of spicy aftershave, although it seemed improbable that even a trace remained after his drenchings. Maybe a really good men's scent permeated the skin and released fragrance almost forever. Or maybe he was just the nicest-smelling man she'd ever met—even wrapped in a fuzzy old blanket. She had an impulse to test her theories by snuggling against his shoulder and nuzzling the hollow of his throat. This situation would be wonderful if she wasn't trying to get a story out of him.

The flickering glow of the lantern was the perfect setting for seduction, and she was a heart-stopping beauty. But Max wasn't about to become romantically involved with a reporter, not even one who'd aroused him with a casual hug. He wanted to tell her to sit still; her squirming was driving him wild. In spite of his best intentions, he'd maneuvered himself closer, his bare arm brushing against her until it seemed only natural to rest it across her shoulders.

"If you don't mind..." he said huskily.

"It certainly is crowded..."

Her hip was against his, and he wasn't quite sure how that had happened.

"I think it's a little quieter now," he said after what seemed an extremely long interval broken only by a few inane remarks. "Surely the storm won't rage like this all night."

He prided himself on self-control, but sitting next to Leigh was a real test of his restraint. The evening was still young, but the space behind the mattress was extremely crowded.

She shifted position at the same moment he did, and somehow they were closer than before, her head cradled on his shoulder, her hair tickling his nose.

"The floor gets hard," she said.

"Yes."

"I suppose we really are safer behind the mattress."

"No doubt."

"That nasty little man should have boarded up his windows, instead of worrying about how much he could charge."

"If he had, we wouldn't need to worry about the windows blowing in."

"Flying glass is a real danger," she said.

He tightened his hold on her shoulder, letting his fingers caress her upper arm. "We're safer here."

Could he sit this way all night, holding her close,

without doing something he'd regret? He tried hard not to think of her as a desirable woman. It wasn't possible. Even if he closed his eyes, he could still sense the heat of her body. The intoxicating scent of her skin was making him light-headed.

She was extraordinary in more ways than appearance and sensuality. How many women had such strong inner resources in a crisis? He had to admit she was quite a woman—still a reporter, but certainly a cut above the tabloid writers. She wouldn't be a bad person to interview him. In fact, she might be in a position to reverse some of the bad press he'd received, especially his playboy reputation.

The wind battering the small cottage was getting to him.

Acting on impulse, he cradled her in both arms, feeling a need to protect her—if only from himself. He had another impulse, risky but potentially helpful. There might be an arrangement that could do both of them some good.

"It won't last forever," he whispered close to her ear. "Why don't you close your eyes and try to get some sleep?"

He shouldn't be holding her, shouldn't feel so content burying his nose in her hair and softly kneading her arm with his fingers. But when she relaxed against him, he felt a contentment that overrode his growing need. It was almost as satisfying as seducing her might be. Almost.

He was paying a price for his tender ministrations, stirred to an arousal that was as untimely as it was unwanted. Why couldn't she be something—anything—besides a reporter?

He distracted himself by mulling over his new idea, trying to find some disadvantages while she lay, drowsy and silent, in his arms. Satisfied he had a sensible, workable plan, he decided to sound her out, give her some time to make a decision. He wasn't a man to hesitate when a good opportunity was in front of him, but he had no intention of pressuring her.

"I didn't fully answer your question," he said.

"My question?" she asked sleepily. It was clear she'd forgotten her quest for tidbits of gossip—for the moment.

"About why I was reading the tabloid." He was committed now. All he had to do was convince her.

"You said it was to check on what they were saying about your cousin."

"Yes, but I probably left you with the impression I was only concerned with her welfare."

"Aren't you?"

"Of course, but I have a selfish reason for being unhappy with her elopement. I'm in the States to look for venture capital. We'd like to lessen Schwanstein's dependence on tourism."

"What does that have to do with your cousin?" She sounded fully awake now.

"Darcy was going to help me—by running interference, you might say."

"In what way?" She shifted slightly; he hoped she wouldn't move away.

"If I travel with a temporary fiancée, it will save me from running a gauntlet of eligible females everywhere I go—"

"You want people to believe you're engaged so you won't be pursued by women?"

"That was the plan before Jose swept Darcy off her feet."

Leigh laughed, relaxing even more in the crook of his arm. "Why don't you get someone else?"

"Potential princesses are in short supply—especially one who wouldn't take the charade too seriously."

"You've just given me a hot lead for a story."

Now he could tell when she was teasing.

"Have you ever considered doing anything besides writing? Say, acting?"

She left his embrace, getting up on her knees and trying to read his face in the gloom.

"Are you asking me...?"

"If you would consider helping me in this, I'll reward you handsomely for your time, and it will be a relatively short trip."

"I wouldn't dream of playing your fiancée for any amount of money."

"Don't misunderstand me. The only requirement would be to appear at public functions with me. I wouldn't presume—I wouldn't expect—What I'm trying to say is, your virtue would be safe with me."

"Oh, no. That's something my grandfather would say. But I get your meaning."

"I want you to know this is strictly a business proposition. If you aren't interested in money..."

"I'll do it."

"You just said—"

"I won't do it for money. I want an exclusive interview with you, one I can be proud of writing. No silly fluff piece or rehashed rumors.

"I haven't granted a formal interview to an American reporter since that false report of an affair with the actress—"

"I know you're justified in resenting an outright lie like that," she interrupted. "But dozens of men have been linked with her. Her name sells papers. You didn't have to take it personally."

"I take my reputation very personally."

"I won't do a hatchet job, but I won't do a vanity

piece, either. If you expect me to make you look like a cross between Sir Galahad and Captain Wonder..."

"Are you good enough to do that?"

She seemed to consider the question for a moment. "Yes, I am."

"Modesty isn't one of your virtues."

"False modesty isn't." She grinned wickedly. "You don't seem to be suffering from low self-esteem yourself."

"No, but I suspect you're going to work on that."

"Will I have the opportunity?"

"Yes. I do have one other stipulation."

"What's that?" she asked.

"You can't use social media for the duration of our engagement."

She paused, considering. "Deal."

"Then I agree to your terms. A serious interview in exchange for posing as my fiancée for a brief period. When I leave for home, you may announce that you terminated the engagement."

"Prince dumped by reporter?"

"If that's how you want to present it."

"I'd rather just fade from the picture. I do have a life of my own."

"You don't already have a fiancé, do you? Or a significant other who might be unduly upset?"

"No, and as luck would have it, my mother just

left for two weeks at my brother's vacation home in the Caribbean. With any luck at all, they won't hear about my 'engagement' until it's over."

Now he did smile. He'd just done an outrageously foolish thing, but he felt good about it.

The wind died down, leaving only the sound of rain beating on the roof. They could leave soon, but he wasn't in any hurry.

## 3

L eigh wondered if the Fairy Godmothers' Union knew about Albert.

At just under six feet, Max's valet weighed in around 240, most of it solid muscle. No doubt he could lay out a would-be attacker as easily as he did the prince's wardrobe. And this was the man who was going to turn her into princess material.

She looked around her suite in the Conquistador Hotel while Albert found an inconspicuous spot to stow her plebeian travel gear. She'd never been in a place that looked less like a hotel room.

Real oil paintings decorated the walls, including one of a Renaissance masked ball, which hung over the bed. The windows had shimmering silver and burgundy draperies, and sliding glass doors led to a balcony with a chaise longue and potted plants.

If this was a dream, she didn't want to wake up.

Yesterday morning she'd been driving through pouring rain on the highway, hoping to catch up with the elusive Prince Maximilian. Twenty-four hours later she was his guest in Paradise Beach and turned over to Albert, who was supposed to transform her from girl reporter to royal bride-to-be.

"If you need anything at all, miss, please call me in room 1210." He managed to give the impression of bowing without actually inclining his top-heavy body. "I'm going to make the arrangements for this afternoon."

"I thought we had to shop."

"Yes, miss. I'll have a luncheon tray sent to your suite, and we'll depart at one o'clock."

His English was as fluent as the prince's, but his accent was much more pronounced. When he said one o'clock, she was pretty sure he meant *exactly one o'clock*. She was trying not to be intimidated, concentrating on his drooping mustache and the thin strands of pale hair carefully plastered to his large skull. But comical he wasn't, not impeccably dressed in a charcoal suit with a black brocade vest, gray silk pinstripe tie and starched white shirt. He made her feel like flotsam washed ashore by the storm.

After a night of restless sleep, mostly spent cowering behind the mattress using Max's shoulder as a pillow, she'd hurriedly gotten ready to leave without benefit of a brush or makeup. By the time the prince made arrangements to have her car towed to a garage and drove them to Paradise Beach, she was grubby enough to deserve Albert's politely masked disdain.

Fortunately, as Max had driven north, the storm damage had lessened. After one minor detour, they arrived in mid-morning with their deal more or less worked out.

He agreed to answer every reasonable question when she interviewed him. In return she had to promise not to tell anyone—with the possible exception of her editor, if necessary—that she was only pretending to be his fiancée.

Of course, she'd have to phone into the office from time to time, but Waverly would have to trust her. She was on to something *big* and that was all she could tell him.

Max had brought up the subject of her wardrobe, or lack thereof, rattling off a list of social engagements that made her head spin. Even if there had been time to go home for more clothes, she was woefully lacking in the ball gown department. She'd adamantly refused to let him buy clothes for her until they reached a compromise: after her stint as his fiancée, the whole wardrobe would go to a charity resale shop.

She had until tomorrow evening to complete her Cinderella transformation. That was where Albert came in. He was serving as combination genie and drill sergeant, preparing her to enter the world of the pampered rich. He was as autocratic as he was well mannered; if he told her to drop to the floor and give him ten pushups, she'd probably have done it.

She rushed to shower and wax—heaven forbid some salesclerk should see her leg stubble. She hoped Albert wouldn't be embarrassed if she wore her midcalf-length rust skirt with a casual top. All she'd brought were work clothes.

After a salad served on a bowl of ice and tiny cucumber sandwiches designed for nibbling, she was as ready as she'd ever be. Albert tapped discreetly on her door at one o'clock—exactly.

She'd never looked at clothes with a man before— at least, not serious have-to-have-an-outfit shopping —but then, she'd never met a gentleman's gentleman before, either.

Albert drove the rented sedan to a complex of stores that were more like cottages in a garden than a shopping mall. She recognized big names on small gold-plated signs—Donna Karan, Ralph Lauren, Calvin Klein. A well-known department store was on a cul-de-sac lined with trendy boutiques whose names passed in a blur.

"Here we are, miss." Albert stopped in front of a stucco building with orange roof tiles. A small nameplate beside the door read: SHE. A green-coated valet opened the door for her and slipped behind the wheel the moment Albert vacated the spot.

If there were other customers, she didn't see them. Most likely a setup this exclusive had patrons or clients, not casual shoppers. Albert presented a gold-bordered business card to an elegant receptionist in black, and she led them into the inner sanctum—the showroom.

The show began. Models paraded in the evening collection while Albert made notes on a pad of paper. At first Leigh was awed by the models themselves, tall winsome beauties who should have something more interesting to do with their afternoons than working as animated clothes dummies. Then she realized Albert was asking her opinion on the dresses.

"I love that chartreuse," she said just to test him.

He didn't bat an eye. "His Highness isn't fond of that shade."

The prince, she learned in the course of the afternoon, also disliked ruffles, platform heels, and double-breasted jackets on women.

Apparently, he was partial to pale peach and ivory undergarments, especially bras that were cleverly underwired to enhance cleavage. She wasn't sure how many items Albert ordered, but she thought she'd sure like to be at the resale shop when this donation came in.

Her feet ached up to her knees, and she longed to duck into the nearest sportswear store and stock up on white T-shirts and jeans. When Albert was finally satisfied, he hustled her back to the Conquistador, where room service delivered her dinner only moments before Hans arrived.

Hans wasn't her dinner companion; he was one of Max's bodyguards, assigned to tutor her on the history and customs of Schwanstein. His Highness had a business function that evening, according to her tutor, a younger blonder version of Albert. Hans seemed pleased that she was a quick learner.

When he finally left, he pushed out the dinner cart, piled high with superfluous plates and metal covers. The garnishes had been impressive—radish roses, sprigs of parsley, orange spirals and lemon slices with designs cut into the rinds. The dinner had been skimpy—broiled chicken breast, spinach salad, and steamed vegetables.

It seemed that Albert had her on a diet. She wasn't pleased. At five foot five, she thought keeping her weight under 130 was reasonable. If that was plump by the prince's standards, he'd only have to put up with it for a little while.

She dug into her duffel and found a foil packet of airline peanuts, then sat cross-legged on the pale-blue bedspread and thoughtfully munched them. She was really in over her head this time. It was one thing to coax interviews from the beautiful people, quite another to pretend she was one of them.

There was more to being a prince's fiancée than wearing a gown with a high-fashion label and knowing the square mileage of Schwanstein.

Where was the prince? His plan had seemed simple when she was with him; now she could see all kinds of complications. How could she face the world feeling like a fraud? Would she be labeled an opportunist?

Would her writing lose credibility just when she was trying to build a reputation for honest, insightful interviews? Saying goodbye to him didn't seem like a snap anymore, either. What if she started liking him —as a person, not a prince?

The only immediate remedy for her doubts was a nice hot bath. She ran water in the big sunken tub, threw in one of the luscious bath bombs the hotel provided, and stepped down into it. There was even a headrest so she could lean back and totally relax.

The hotel phone disturbed a hazy dream. She'd dozed off in the tub, and someone wasn't about to hang up. Her first impulse was to jump out and race to the desk in the outer room of the suite, but it wasn't necessary. There was a phone within reach on a recessed shelf running the length of the pale-green tiled wall. She reached above her head and grasped the receiver.

"Hello?"

"Did I wake you?"

There was no mistaking the prince's voice.

"No, I was taking a bath." She still had a hard time calling him Max, but Your Highness seemed too stuffy for a fiancé.

"Would it be all right if I came to your suite just for a few minutes?" he asked.

"Sure."

"I'll be right there."

He didn't say goodbye. She belatedly realized she should have asked for time to get dressed. Hearing his voice when she was sleepy and off guard had been like feeling a mild current of electricity passing through the bath. She tingled from her shoulders to her toes.

No time to panic. She scrambled out and grabbed a thick white towel, losing herself in several yards of incredibly plush terry.

This hotel thought of everything—a robe made of the same luxurious cloth was neatly folded beside the stacks of spare towels. She slipped into it and securely knotted the belt, trying to think of what to wear as she finished drying her puckered toes.

She made it as far as the bedroom when she heard a knock—three firm measured taps. Her face was flushed from the heat of the bath, and her hair hung down to her shoulders in complete disarray.

Remember, this is only a business arrangement, she told herself as she rushed barefoot to the door, then took a deep breath and opened it without thinking to look through the peephole.

"Good evening." He smiled, and the warmth of the smile reached his eyes.

"Hi."

She stepped back, floored by the man who stepped into the room. He cut a dashing princely figure in midnight-black formal wear. His black tie was loose, hanging askew against the sharp pleats of his shirt, and his jaw was lightly shadowed. He looked rakish and a bit tired, but so handsome he literally left her speechless.

"I thought there were a few things we should go over before tomorrow evening." He closed the door behind him.

She nodded, fighting an impulse to curtsy. He wasn't Max anymore; he was Maximilian of Schwanstein, a prince from his dark-mahogany hair to the mirrorlike surface of his patent-leather shoes.

"Are you pleased with your wardrobe?" Max asked, feeling awkward in the presence of a member of the opposite sex for the first time in years.

"Not entirely."

He raised his eyebrows, surprised that Albert had failed to accommodate her tastes.

"If you don't have something you need..."

"No, that's not the trouble. I have too much. We'll be traveling, so I can wear the same dresses in different cities. It's a terrible waste, buying so much..."

He laughed softly, amused and pleased by her thrifty nature and entranced by her pink-cheeked earnestness.

The robe was much too large, enveloping her in its folds and revealing nothing of the curvaceous beauty of her body. Perhaps because he had to use his imagination, she seemed all the more desirable. He wanted to untie the sash she was worrying between her thumb and forefinger and peel back the thick layer of cloth.

What had possessed him when he promised not to seduce her? His fingers were charged with the urge to reach inside her chaste white cocoon and caress the swell of her luscious breasts. The real waste wasn't buying her too much; it was being honor-bound not to take advantage of their arrangement.

"Albert could return the black column dress—it's probably too tight, anyway. And I certainly won't need four dinner suits."

"Poor Albert. You rejected half of what he chose for you, and I berated him for being so stingy."

"You didn't!"

"Don't worry. He's been with me more than half my life, and he's usually the one who does the scolding."

"I guess I can believe that. He is a bit— He was very nice to me."

She shrugged, clearly making a conscious choice not to criticize his valet. This, too, pleased him.

"Were you going to say 'intimidating'?" Max laughed again, relaxing for the first time since he'd begun his long day of social and business obligations. "I can't believe a reporter would be cowed by Albert."

"I'm not," she quickly denied, her eyes meeting his, the depths sparkling in a sudden burst of mischief. "In fact, I think you should punish him by making him eat the meals he's been ordering for me. He's trying to shrink me to a size two by tomorrow night, I think."

"I'll mention it to him."

"No! He worked so hard today, I wouldn't want to offend him."

Once again Max laughed, and he wondered why everything she said amused him. He was world-weary and jaded, perhaps too inclined to see the baser side of people's motives. Why did she have this effect on him, like a cool breeze blowing off the lake behind his family's palace?

"It's better to avoid offending Albert. I depend on him not to let me wear navy socks with black trousers."

What an idiotic thing to say. He was trying to impress her with lighthearted banter, which wasn't his style. He touched his bottom lip with his tongue, wanting to sample the sweetness of her mouth but held back by his own word. He'd been a fool to offer assurances she hadn't requested. His groin ached just thinking of what might have been.

"I'm sorry about this robe. I'm not exactly dressed for company." She gave him a little smile that was anything but apologetic. He was the one intruding on her privacy.

"I'll have an itinerary for you tomorrow, but I thought you might like to know my plans—our plans —for our first public appearance."

"Yes, please."

He dropped his gaze, only to become enchanted

by her shapely ankles and slender feet. They were still slightly pink from the bath. He caught a faint scent of jasmine and inhaled deeply.

"I didn't ask Albert about perfume. Did you find something to your liking?"

"You don't need to buy me any. I have some of my favorite with me—Waterlily."

"I'm not familiar with it. You'll have an opportunity to make some selections at the spa tomorrow."

"The spa?"

"That's the message from Albert. He's ordered a six a.m. wake-up call and a makeover day. We have to leave the hotel at seven forty tomorrow evening. Our debut will be informal. One of your cocktail dresses will be appropriate."

"About all those clothes..."

"How can you, a reporter, forget about the press?"

"Pictures?" She seemed to shrink in the oversized wrap.

"Pictures." He smiled wickedly. "Sleep well, my love."

She pouted at the closed door after he left, not appreciating his flippant use of the endearment. Of course, he was only trying it out, practicing for his role as her fiancé, but it annoyed her immensely. When a man called her his love, she wanted him to mean it.

She slept just fine—from three to six a.m. Tossing and turning before that, she'd thought about the next day with foreboding. She wavered between running away in the night and telling Max she'd changed her mind.

She did neither. They had a deal, and for better or worse, she was a woman of her word. She was stuck.

At least Albert didn't personally supervise her makeover. He did show up at exactly seven a.m. to escort her to the faux-marble splendor of the Conquistador's torture chamber for women. There he turned her over to Miss Yvonne, who promised to pamper her as only the spa could. Since Leigh's idea of pampering was sleeping until noon, then eating cold pizza washed down by a diet cola, they didn't engage in much sparkling conversation.

She did manage to snatch a few short naps as she endured the exotic rites: a eucalyptus steam bath, an herbal wrap, aromatherapy, reflexology, and some therapeutic yoga thrown in for good measure. Her masseuse, Olga, soon made her long for Albert; at least he didn't knead her like bread dough.

Escorted from one curtained station to the next, she caught only glimpses of the spa's rich and famous patrons, their modesty preserved in the same pink cotton robes that she wore. Enthusiastic practitioners of the beautician's arts repeatedly assured her that her skin would feel like velvet.

After a luncheon that made Albert's selections seem generous, she was led to the roof of the hotel for her air bath wearing only little paper slippers and a pink towel. Here the spa's patrons weren't segregated from each other.

She recognized the ex-wife of an American millionaire and the alleged mistress of an internationally acclaimed opera star, and she saw far more of them than she cared to. The women were sunning their well-oiled bodies stark naked.

Overhead the sky was blue and empty, but it didn't take much imagination to visualize a fleet of low-flying helicopters hovering over the roof. It would be the ultimate in aerial tours.

She declined to drop her towel. She was the only woman still wearing one, but she wasn't getting naked with a bunch of bare-bottomed strangers.

The hairdresser was Mr. Melvin, and he really knew his stuff. He trimmed and tamed her hair, working like part of a surgical team with a colorist and an eyebrow specialist. Leigh couldn't disapprove of the results—a stunningly elaborate upsweep. Her own mother wouldn't have recognized her.

When she was finally discharged from the

makeover mill, her pink nails sparkled like polished gemstones, and her skin had a radiant glow, artfully produced by the makeup consultant.

Her outfit for the evening was a periwinkle dinner dress, scoop-necked in front and plunging nearly to her waist in back, with long sleeves and a minimal skirt. She was mildly embarrassed to see that Albert had laid out everything—one of the underwired ivory bras, nude panty hose, pearl-gray clutch purse and matching heels. Panties were conspicuously absent.

Was the valet reticent about handling them, or did he think she should go without in the interest of avoiding panty lines?

She pulled out deep mahogany veneered drawers until she found her new undergarments, folded and lined up with military precision. Some things a woman had to decide for herself.

She was ready early but couldn't sit still. Expecting to be fetched by Albert, she heard a muffled knock, three evenly spaced taps, neither overbearing nor impatient. After counting slowly to ten so she wouldn't appear too eager, she sauntered over and opened the door.

Max was standing in the corridor, solemn-faced and silent, elegant in a smoky-gray silk suit with an off-white shirt and a marbled dove-and-charcoal tie.

She said the first thing that came to mind. "Good grief, we're color-coordinated."

He slowly studied her from head to toe, grinning when he saw that the dove-gray leather of her pumps was identical to one of the shades in his tie.

"Albert does have a good eye for color." He threw dignity to the wind, lifted one foot and hiked up his trouser leg to display his woven silk hosiery.

She laughed, a soft, pretty sound that broke down the wall of reserve between them and brought a broad smile to his face.

"You're ravishing tonight, Miss Leigh Bailey," he said, taking her hand in his and lightly touching his lips to her fingertips.

"I'm having a hard time remembering who I am; so many people have worked on me today."

"I'll remember for you. You're beautiful tonight, but no more so than when I first saw you standing in the rain."

"Your Highness, you take my breath away."

"If you call me anything but Max, you'll incur my royal wrath. I'll be forced to punish you."

"I'm not sure you have jurisdiction here."

Her eyes sparkled in a way that had nothing to do

with the art of cosmetology. For perhaps the first time in his life, Max wished he did have the power of a royal despot. There were things he wanted to do to this American that had nothing to do with punishment and everything to do with pleasure.

"I'm a guest in your country," he said, offering her his arm. "I will endeavor to observe your laws and traditions."

"That's encouraging." She smiled, and he felt warm all over.

He wasn't displeased when the lift was slow in coming. In fact, he was sorry it was an express. He would have liked to prolong this brief time together. They rode down to the lobby in comfortable silence. After a day filled with incessant talk, it was restful to be with a woman who didn't feel compelled to fill every quiet moment with chatter. Being with her restored his energy level and left him pleasantly relaxed.

Leigh was an unusual woman. No one who saw her could doubt her suitability as a prince's fiancée. Darcy had done him a favor by eloping with the bullfighter, and fate had smiled when he'd tried to read Leigh's bumper sticker.

The paparazzi were lying in wait on the street outside the mansion where Mr. and Mrs. Charles Braeworthy were waiting to introduce the prince to their closest friends and business associates at a small dinner party.

Albert was doubling as chauffeur, followed in another car by Hans and the other bodyguard, whose name Leigh didn't know. She rode in the back seat, only a hand's span apart from the prince—from Max. She had to remember to call him Max.

"Your peers are waiting," he teased, obviously enjoying the fact that she'd have to run the gauntlet of news-hungry reporters with him.

"I'm sure they're mostly local. Anyway, *Celebrity* magazine interviews by appointment," she said in a tone intended to put him in his place. "I'm afraid you're big news only in Paradise Beach—and in the tabloids."

"Now," he said ominously. "Walk quickly."

She thrust out her chin defiantly. She wasn't going to be intimidated by the crowd of photographers and reporters she saw through the window.

The sedan entered a circular drive, followed by the news corps on foot, and eased to a stop outside a door flanked by carriage lights on poles. Leigh got a fleeting impression of shutters and brick, then Albert was opening the door, offering his hand as she stepped out.

Max moved fast, joining her on the pavement as a miniature lightning storm of flashbulbs went off in her face. She expected him to grab her arm and hustle her into the house.

She didn't expect him to grab both her shoulders and kiss her soundly on her carefully lined and made-up lips.

She saw stars, but she couldn't pinpoint their origin — the sky, the cameras, or her own mind. It took every shred of willpower not to put a hand over her mouth and lock in the pulsing sensation left by his kiss.

"Darling, our hosts are waiting for us," he said, the amusement in his voice rippling through her, making her realize she was frozen to the spot in shock.

He put his hand on her waist, low on her waist, and gently propelled her toward the dark Georgian-style door. She walked, but only after his fingers nudged her just enough to suggest she might need a pinch to wake up.

Then they were inside. He was too busy being greeted to apologize for the very public, very energetic kiss—if he had any intention of doing so. Her lips were still tingling.

"I'm deeply honored," he was saying to a portly woman with iron-gray curls and a dark-red dress adorned with what appeared to be heirloom diamonds—large, gaudy, and set in a necklace inspired by the jeweled collars found in Egyptian tombs. "Allow me to present Miss Leigh Bailey."

He didn't explain her; she liked that. He did increase the pressure of his hand on her waist, giving her a cue to say something. She didn't like his hint; she wasn't an idiot.

Smiling broadly, she pressed Mrs. Braeworthy's moist plump hand and made what she hoped was an appropriate comment about her heavy necklace. Either her hostess was inordinately proud of it or just thrilled to have real royalty in her house. She beamed.

"Please call me Marty, short for Martha," she trilled. "All my friends do."

"I'm Leigh—short already."

Mrs. Braeworthy's husband rumbled with laughter; apparently he had a sense of humor. Leigh decided to treat them the way she did her great-uncle Calvin and his fourth wife, a technique that usually endeared her to the old boys without annoying their wives.

She could handle this hobnobbing; it was a challenge, but she was going to keep her end of the bargain even if she had to imitate Princess Di. She sailed through the introductions—smiling broadly and making small talk. Max took his hand away; apparently the baby bird was ready to fly on her own.

Four hours later she was more in the mood for crawling—home.

"This is hard work," she whispered to Max in one of their few moments alone.

He laughed; he was doing that a lot lately.

Dinner was over, but the after-dinner drinks kept coming. So did guests who were either late for the meal or not important enough to feed. Leigh suspected the latter. She even recognized someone among the latest arrivals, a supermodel she'd interviewed just last year whose one-word moniker—Natasha—matched her sophistication.

"There's actually someone here I can introduce to you," she said, taking Max's arm and steering him toward the willowy raven-haired model.

"Natasha, I'm Leigh Bailey, *Celebrity* magazine," she said just to avoid the embarrassment of not being recognized in her princess getup.

"Of course, I adored your article—and I forgive you for using that dreadful photo with my hair all kinky."

"This is Prince Maximilian," Leigh said, telling herself it was silly to feel so darn proud of being on his arm.

"Max, darling!" Natasha inclined her long body in his direction and kissed him full on the mouth.

Leigh felt invisible all of a sudden. "So you two already know each other."

"We met at a wonderful ski jaunt in the Alps," Natasha said without looking at her.

"Yes, the Duke of Cornelli was our host," Max said for Leigh's benefit, since the model already knew it. "You're looking marvelous, Natasha."

"I'm not feeling marvelous. That nasty storm ruined my week—but of course, you know that."

"It will spice up your memoirs to include a hurricane," Max said.

"Darling, my memoirs are spicy enough already, as you well know."

Leigh didn't doubt it. This was definitely the longest evening of her life.

Finally, her big debut was over.

Max was quiet on the ride back to the hotel. Now that she thought about it, he'd been quiet before they got to the dinner party, too. Why should she be surprised? Why would a prince want to talk to her? She was the enemy, a reporter. He was only with her because it was the lesser of two evils: fending off hordes of eligible women or putting up with her.

He'd done more than put up with Natasha. They'd

talked earnestly, alone in a corner, until other guests demanded his attention.

Max rested his head on the back of the seat, willing enough to let Albert find the way back to the hotel. Clouds obscured the moon, and the velvety darkness allowed him to watch Leigh without being obvious.

Natasha had been miffed, especially when he ignored her questions and refused to explain why he'd escorted Leigh to the party. He had enough male ego to enjoy her ire, especially since Leigh's elegance had overshadowed the almond-eyed model's.

He'd found a rain-soaked water sprite and transformed her into a fairy princess. He smiled at the fanciful notion, but he had misgivings. His plan was simple enough: use a decoy to fend off predatory females. His feelings about her were more complex.

He inhaled deeply, letting her subtle scent tease his senses. She'd worn her own perfume, instead of selecting one at the spa, and he realized how wise she was. It suited her, suggesting the freshness of a rain-washed summer garden. Did she splash it on her wrists or dab it behind her delicate earlobes? He wanted to search for the source with his nostrils and his tongue.

He took another deep breath, this time trying to concentrate on more mundane thoughts—the hidden agenda of his host and the possibility of interesting Braeworthy in Schwanstein investments.

Albert stopped the car under the front canopy of the Conquistador, but Max didn't give him time to open the door for him.

"I'll see Miss Bailey to her room," he said. "I won't need the car again tonight."

Leigh felt something suspiciously like relief. She'd had an unsettling hunch that Max might deposit her at the hotel and seek out a more exciting companion for the rest of the night. Natasha, for instance. It was none of her business, but...

The elevator was waiting for them, the door open. It carried them up to her floor with the speed of a rocket launched into space. Before they'd done more than exchange tentative smiles, they were standing in front of her door.

"I'm afraid this evening wasn't much fun for you," he said, looking into her eyes without the sardonic smile he usually seemed to reserve for their moments alone.

"It was interesting."

"Interesting. Hmm. You're a writer. You can be more descriptive than that. It was a bloody bore, and you know it."

"For you, maybe. I enjoy meeting people."

"Do you?"

He lightly stroked the underside of her chin with one long tanned finger. She clenched her jaw, not wanting him to detect the involuntary quiver he was causing.

"You look lovely. I was proud to be with you this evening," he murmured.

"The spa did wonders."

"The spa provided something for you to do while I attended tedious business meetings. The beauty business is dedicated to making women look alike. Fortunately, you defeated their best efforts. Your beauty is unique."

Now she did feel shivery. She knew Max could be charming, but his words washed over her like the stardust in animated fairy tales.

"Good night, Leigh."

His face was only inches away, his dark eyes focused on hers. For one heady moment she thought he was going to kiss her. Then he turned and strode down the corridor without another word.

She held the keycard in her hand a long time before she opened the door.

## 4

Albert provided the itinerary along with a huge breakfast—Max must have said something to him—and the morning newspapers. The pleasure of rising late and enjoying gourmet coffee, exotic fruit, and eggs Benedict paled when Leigh saw the front-page headline:

**_Prince Squires American Beauty._**

At least the local photographer had missed the kiss. Or the paper had chosen not to run it, possibly because the conservative old-money readers in Paradise Beach preferred their gossip served up as discreet innuendoes.

Was Marty Braeworthy even now manning a hotline, dishing out the true story to those among her nearest and dearest friends who hadn't merited an invitation to the party?

Leigh stared moodily at the fuzzy image of Max with his arm around her waist, hustling her toward the mansion. She did look good. In fact, her own mother probably wouldn't recognize her in the picture. She ran her fingers through hair that was now flat and stiff, looking forward to doing it her way again—if Albert didn't object.

What would her friends think? Her editor? For that matter, how did she feel about this surreal plunge into the world of the rich and royal?

She touched her chin where the prince's finger had stroked her, wondering how it would feel to have his lips trace a path along her throat, his breath warm on her skin— The phone rang, and she reached over her breakfast tray to pick up the nearest of the six or so phones in her suite.

"Hello."

"Waverly here. Is this Bailey?"

"Yes."

She pretended to herself she wasn't disappointed. She had no reason to hope Max might be calling.

"What's new with the prince? I saw the *Trib*."

So everyone in Miami knew about her romp with royalty.

"You know better than to believe everything you read in the papers," she told her editor. Max hadn't been happy, but she'd had to let Waverly in on their plan. He was still her boss.

"That's what I figured," he said with a knowing laugh. "Well, keep me posted."

"Sure."

She'd like to post him all right—via the U.S. Postal Service to the Antarctic. Was it so far-fetched to believe a prince might date her because he liked her?

Yes, she admitted glumly, it was. So, what was on the itinerary for today?

The schedule she pulled from a heavy nine-by-twelve envelope was impressive, printed on thick paper with a gold-embossed royal seal.

Not only had the valet listed events, locations and times, he'd included suggestions that she took as orders on what to wear. At noon she was supposed to wear a bathing suit under the turquoise-and-black-striped beach coat, a wardrobe oddity she hadn't really expected to need.

Skimming through the list, she concluded that her main function was to wear different outfits. Max might as well have hired a model—or wagged his little finger at Natasha, who'd probably turn somer-saults for the chance to grab headlines with His Highness.

"It'll be the best story I've written—maybe the

best royal profile ever," she said, reminding herself of the reason she was doing this.

So why did she feel so gloomy?

She was ready when the tap came on the door. Albert was five minutes early.

"I hope you like smoked salmon and mimosas," Max said when she opened the door.

He grinned boyishly, shifting the handle of a big plastic cooler from one hand to the other.

"I was expecting Albert." What a dumb thing to say.

"I'm sorry to disappoint you."

"Believe me, you haven't."

Great, admit he makes your pulse pound like conga drums, she admonished herself, taking in his loose-fitting yellow-and-white soccer jersey and dark-green shorts that left most of his muscular thighs bare. He was wearing sandals and had one of the hotel's huge white towels draped on his shoulder. Were they really going swimming?

"A friend made arrangements for us to use a private beach—just the kind of secluded place lovers would choose," he said with a mischievous sparkle in his eyes.

"According to the itinerary, we're supposed to frolic for the press?"

"Don't worry, we won't elude anybody. No one will

doubt we're involved in a relationship." He put his hand under her elbow after she closed the door behind them. "You have no idea what peace of mind that gives me."

"No, I don't," she said dryly, remembering the dark-haired model and her big openmouthed kiss.

A long gray stretch limo was parked in front of the hotel, but she looked in both directions for his rental sedan.

"Here," he said, leading her to the limo. "Since you left yours at home…"

He was smiling. At least he had a sense of humor.

"I thought I'd have to get married to ride in one of these," she said, sinking back on the plush seat and taking in some of the perks: TV, stereo, cellular phone, smoky-gray windows, and a bar with an ice bucket.

Max disapproved of the plastic goblets furnished by the service, but the combination of French champagne and Florida orange juice made the best mimosa he'd ever tasted—or maybe Leigh's enthusiasm gave it a special zing. He settled down beside her, draping his arm on the seat behind her.

"I don't think snuggling is part of our deal," she said, sliding a few inches away from him.

He liked feeling her shoulder against his arm and her thigh against his. He had no intention of chasing her around the back of the limo, but her flowery perfume was making him light-headed. He was used to women who had fragrances blended especially for them, but never with such appealing results.

The walkie-talkie concealed under the towel he'd dropped on the seat crackled unexpectedly, giving her a start.

"Sorry, just Hans checking in," he said. "My men are following the cars following us."

"Are you sure we're just going to the beach? This sounds like a spy mission."

"This, Leigh, is how I live—at least whenever I leave Schwanstein. My own people tend to take me for granted."

"No mothers lining up to have you pat their babies' heads? No fair maidens kneeling to kiss your ring?"

"Alas, none."

"I'm disillusioned." She grinned wickedly. "Next you'll tell me you don't live in a castle."

"I don't. My ancestors abandoned ours in the eighteenth century, I'm happy to say. All the water had to be hauled up a mountain, so it was a singularly inconvenient fortress."

"Then where do you live?"

"My father and I share the palace. There are twenty-two bedrooms, but still it sometimes seems confining. Do you live with your family?"

"I share the city of Miami with my mother—and sometimes it's not big enough for the two of us."

He laughed, but a nagging doubt persisted: could a woman this beautiful be wholly unattached?

"Perhaps when I'm a father, I'll understand the parental urge to control my offsprings' lives," he mused, forgetting the plastic goblet in his hand.

"My mother isn't controlling, just inquisitive. If I have lunch with a business acquaintance, she wants his life history."

"My father would like an international hotline on single females—an Interpol dating service."

She sipped her mimosa, enjoying it without making silly comments about bubbles or drinking before noon. Everything she said interested him because she never uttered the obvious. He silently cursed the parasites who would be stalking their picnic on the beach. He yearned for time alone with Leigh.

"Actually, I admire my mother immensely," she said. "When my father deserted us—did I mention I haven't even met his fourth wife?—my mother lost a pretty cushy lifestyle. Country clubs, live-in help, the social whirl... All she had left was my brother, me, and an art-history degree. The only job she'd ever had was camp counselor."

"Surely your father provided for you?"

"Yes, but trophy wives are expensive, so his help was minimal. My mother, though, went into real estate and made a big success of it by giving high-class service to owners of low-cost homes. In some areas she has so many FOR SALE signs, it looks like she's running for office."

"She sounds remarkable. My mother would have admired her. She put a great deal of time and energy into helping people."

"I read about her accident, of course. She must have been a special person."

"She was."

The limo left the heavy traffic and slowed, according to his instructions. Since he had to feed the barracudas, he didn't want any delays because they'd lost his vehicle.

The walkie-talkie crackled again; Hans reported the press was still on his tail.

Leigh refused a refill, wanting to stay alert. This was the best date she'd ever had: champagne, a limo, and a man with ballroom manners and bedroom eyes. Too bad it was only pretend. But while it lasted, she was going to savor every beautiful moment.

Somewhere along their route, the space between them had vanished. She was keenly aware of his hip and thigh against hers, and his aftershave teased her nostrils, reminding her of The Kiss. If getting engaged to the prince meant an occasional lip-lock, she was ready, willing, and eager. She'd never been kissed that way.

Did Europeans have a special technique, or was it Max's natural gift? She got goosebumps just remembering the way his mouth had covered hers, making her lips tingle and taking her breath away.

His first kiss—and a public one at that—had the impact of a dynamite charge. How would it feel to be kissed by him for real?

She imagined mushroom clouds and erupting volcanoes, then the limo slowed and entered one of the high-security oceanside estates. They were waved through a gate by a green-shirted private security guard.

"How will the reporters and photographers get through security?" she asked.

"They won't." He laughed softly, enjoying a private

joke. "But they can park about a mile away and hike a rugged obstacle course along the beach. If they don't fall in the ocean or break their cameras on the concrete barrier that blocks off this section of beach, they'll be able to use their telephoto lenses. You may want to wear the top of your bathing suit."

"You bet I'll wear it!"

"I forgot—Americans can still be prudish about such things. If we were doing this on a European beach, you would certainly be topless."

"I don't think so."

"Don't be sure until you've experienced the sun caressing your bare back and the sea breeze rippling over your breasts."

He grinned, and she felt like squirming. He was talking about sun and wind, but she was imagining hands and lips.

"Our host is away, so we can go right to the beach," Max said when the limo stopped some distance from a huge gleaming white house set in a grove of trees. "We can walk from here."

The bodyguards hadn't followed them onto the estate, and their driver showed no sign of leaving the vicinity of the limo. Max carried the cooler and big towel and led the way.

Leigh had lived most of her life near the ocean, but this beach took her breath away. It had the pearl-white sand, swaying palms, and azure water of a travel poster, with the seclusion of an uncharted island. Shells and bits of driftwood were scattered at random, gifts from the sea that were usually gathered by tourists on the public beaches.

"This is lovely. It's hard to believe we're not completely alone," she said.

"Believe me, the cameras will find us."

He stopped a few dozen feet from the darker wave-washed sand near the water and set the cooler down, then let the wind unfurl the towel before he spread it.

"Is this satisfactory?" he asked, starting to pull his shirt over his head.

"Yes, very."

One spot on the sand was much like another, but the chest he revealed would be unique on any beach. She tried not to stare, but pecs like his were mesmerizing, sun-bronzed with a sprinkling of fine dark hair and chocolate-brown nipples she could practically taste.

He turned his back to unzip, letting his shorts fall to his ankles, and gracefully stepped out of them. She'd seen quite a bit of him in his fuzzy blanket, but his idea of a swimsuit was a scrap of sea-foam-green jersey that exposed more than it covered.

The royal buttocks didn't disappoint. They were

firm and rounded and perfect for stroking. She swallowed hard and turned her back.

"Let me help you." He put his hands on her shoulders, but she was clutching the front of the beach coat. "You *are* wearing a bathing suit, aren't you?"

"Oh, yes. I followed Albert's instructions."

He was waiting. She could disrobe or engage in a tug-of-war. She felt about as sophisticated as the waitresses at Rocky's Roadhouse on the old highway west of Miami, and they wore pigtails and off-the-shoulder peasant blouses.

She let go of the fistful of silky material and felt warmth on her bare shoulders as he peeled away the beach coat.

It wasn't the sun; it was his breath, hot and tickling as he gently nuzzled the back of her neck.

"Albert made me buy it," she said, looking down and realizing just how little there was of her silver bikini. "I'll see he's suitably rewarded."

He rested his hands on her waist, and she didn't know whether to be sensible or sensual, to pull away or move closer. He made the choice harder when he slid his hands down the bare sides of her hips in an outrageously intimate caress.

"My mother doesn't know I'm here. If this makes page one in a tabloid..."

"You're absolutely right." He pulled away but not before playfully hugging her.

"Oh."

"Come on." He took her hand and pulled her toward the water, pausing so she could slip out of her flip-flops before they ran into the ocean.

The sea was relatively calm, making it easy to forget about hurricanes and giant waves. He released her hand and plunged into the swell, staying under so long she began to worry. She could see the headline: **Prince Lost at Sea.** But she didn't give a darn about his fame; she just wanted to see that sexy smile again.

"Max! Max!"

She started swimming in the same direction, but the ocean had swallowed him up. Looking back, she could see the shoreline was farther away than she liked. She was a good pool swimmer, but she had a healthy respect for the ocean. There was no sign of him.

A sudden tug on her ankle pulled her under. She struggled, but it took only an instant to realize she wasn't in danger—of drowning. When she bobbed to the surface, her face was only inches from his.

"You scared me!" She twisted away from his hands when he tried to rest them on her shoulders.

"I'm sorry. I thought you'd know it was me," he said contritely.

"I did—but I thought you were drowning. You hadn't come up..."

"Would you be sorry if I did drown?" He closed in on her, locking his hands behind her neck. "Would you miss me?"

Miss him? She didn't have an answer, not one she was able to give him.

She was in over her head and sinking fast, but it had nothing to do with swimming. Max put his arms around her, and they plunged to the bottom. His lips found hers. And stayed there as they rose to the surface together.

"One not for the cameras," he murmured, holding her close and treading water for both of them as his mouth found hers again.

She shut her eyes and trusted him. All the feeling in her body was concentrated in the area he was caressing with parted lips. His tongue touched hers, then plunged deep, making stars explode behind her closed lids.

"Whoa!"

"I take that as a compliment," he said, holding her against him.

"We should go back to shore."

She was terrified. And not of any ocean predators. What if she fell for Max? He was a prince, and she was the girl who'd vowed never to be dependent on a man. Her picture-perfect childhood had turned into a nightmare when her mother suddenly had to cope alone. Leigh was never going to get caught in the trap of arranging her whole life for a man. Not that Max would ever see her as a potential princess.

She didn't want the playboy prince complicating her life. Swimming back to the beach, she hoped it wasn't too late to avoid an emotional entanglement.

He followed her to their towel and produced another smaller one, watching silently while she dried her face and arms.

"If I did frighten you, I'm sorry. It wasn't my intention," he said.

"We have a business arrangement. You're not supposed to have intentions," she said more sharply than she'd intended.

"I think you've been reading too many tabloids. You believe I do nothing but seduce women."

"I'm sure you do other things, too." She furiously toweled her hair, keeping her face averted.

"Too? As in also? Meaning you think seduction is my main occupation?"

"Oh, don't be so dramatic, Max. I'm not passing judgment on your love life."

"Thank you for that," he said dryly. "Especially since you know absolutely nothing about it. But you are a reporter, aren't you? Playing fast and loose with the facts is a job requirement."

"That's a mean thing to say. Maybe you have too many people fawning over you to—"

"Fawning?" He lowered his voice, sounding dangerously provoked. "People respect me because I respect them."

"Do you respect me?"

He stared at her for a long moment. Then, to her relief, a faint smile replaced his frown. "I believe I do."

Did he deserve his playboy reputation? Max didn't think a healthy interest in the opposite sex was a character flaw. But it still bothered him that Leigh might believe the lurid headlines that sensationalized even his casual friendships with women.

"Maybe I overreacted," she said with a charming little grin.

"Or maybe you're afraid you'll grow to like my kisses." He used a teasing tone, but he really wanted to know how she felt.

"I do like them."

He smiled at her frank admission and liked her even more because of it. A little pretense added spice to a relationship, but lately he'd been put off by coy, manipulative women. That was why he'd persuaded Leigh to run interference for him on this trip.

"Don't turn around, but I think I saw a glint of something," she warned.

"Our friends with the cameras?"

"Yes, now I'm sure."

"Then it's time." He retrieved a plastic bottle from the cooler. "Shall I do the honors, or do you want to?"

"Rub lotion on your back?" She sounded dubious.

"Rub it wherever you choose."

"Okay, I'll do it. Sit."

She knelt behind him, and he could hear the plop as she squeezed the bottle.

"I got too much. It's cold from the cooler. You might not like this."

"Nobody else will know that," he assured her.

"Well, here goes."

He'd never had a less romantic back rub. She slapped it on with the same technique a baker used to knead bread, and her hand hadn't warmed it enough to feel good.

"I have enough in my hand to grease a hippo," she complained. "It's squirting between my fingers."

He reached back and captured her slippery hand, guiding it over his throat and through the mat of hair on his chest, then pressed it against his cheek.

"Have I solved your problem?"

She murmured assent and tried to pull her hand away. He wasn't ready to give it back.

"Lotion applied," she said hoarsely.

"You don't seem to have much practice at this sort of thing." His lips caressed the inner side of her wrist, definitely not part of his plan, but deeply pleasurable.

"My hand, please."

"Of course." He released it, trailing his fingertips down the length of her arm as she pulled away. "Now lie on your stomach, and I'll show you how it's done."

"No, I don't think so."

"Do you want our observers to think I'm a chauvinist, enjoying your ministrations without giving you protection from the rays of the sun?"

"Next you'll say it's part of our deal," she complained, not as reluctant as she pretended.

The towel was warm, and the sand shifted comfortably under her. Max positioned himself to block her from the telephoto lenses; so much for performing for the press. She should call him on it, but the sea breezes made her lethargic. She burrowed into her resting place and sighed under his touch.

"You really are good at this," she said as he slowly and thoroughly went from her shoulders to her waist.

"Shall I go on?" he asked.

"Please do."

She'd hate herself later. Right now, his hands felt wonderful. She practically squirmed with pleasure as he worked his way down to her toes.

"You won't burn now."

He was wrong. He'd ignited her senses, and she was getting hotter by the moment.

"Now what we came for," he said, rising to his feet.

Such nice feet, too, lean and tanned and only inches from her face. Knots of muscle swelled the backs of his calves without looking lumpy. Didn't the man have any defects?

"Lunch," he announced.

"Maybe after a little nap."

"If I lie down beside you, Miss Bailey," he said in a low caressing voice, "you won't want your mother to see the photographs."

"I hate cameras," she said under her breath, sitting up and casting aside her mood of drowsy contentment.

"Open your mouth," he ordered.

"Why?"

"Because I'm a prince, and I've commanded you to do so," he teased, holding up a cluster of plump purple grapes.

"In that case..." She closed her eyes and let him lay one on her tongue, biting into the juicy fruit with zest. "Wonderful."

"Now feed me," he prompted.

"This is just for the photographers, right?"

"Just for them."

"Okay."

He handed her a flat plastic container of canapes —bits of smoked salmon and cheese on dainty little crackers. She picked one at random and put it between his lips, surprised when they closed around her fingers and suckled the tips.

"You're a big boy—you can feed yourself," she admonished, but she was already reaching for another tidbit.

She didn't have a chance to give it to him. He lowered his head and kissed her, letting his tongue part her lips. She knew happily-ever-after endings were for other women, but what could it hurt to pretend just for a few minutes that this was real? That a real prince was devouring her mouth because he really wanted to kiss her?

Max closed his eyes and tried to wish away the hidden newshounds. He wanted to be on a secluded beach with Leigh, wanted her all to himself without considering the consequences.

He savored her lips with his, probing deeper into the warmth and sweetness of her mouth.

"Is that enough?" she asked just when he'd decided he never wanted to stop.

He looked into her face and saw nothing but warmth and responsiveness. Women were never more beautiful than when their mouths were swollen and their eyes dewy with passion, and she was so lovely his throat ached. He allowed himself another moment to savor the magic of being with her, then reluctantly stepped away. It was time to leave.

## 5

"One of my bags is missing," Leigh said, studying the luggage cart just wheeled into the room.

"That's all there was, ma'am."

The bellhop had bodybuilder's shoulders and surfer-boy good looks. He was probably only doing this job until fame and fortune beckoned, but he wasn't doing it very well at the moment.

"I saw it on the cart in the lobby. All five bags were on it." She secretly believed anyone who hauled around that many deserved to lose one now and then, but the missing garment bag held evening gowns, including the one she intended to wear for the engagement announcement tonight.

"I'll check for you. It may be on another cart," he

offered with drilled-in courtesy, but not before she saw a frown of annoyance.

"It's like these two," she said, pointing at the two black pieces Albert had provided to carry her temporary wardrobe. "My name is on the tag—Leigh Bailey."

"Yes, ma'am. I'll check at the desk."

"Please do it right away."

She tipped him five times what he deserved, knowing it was only the minimum at the Jefferson Arms, one of Chicago's older but luxurious downtown hotels. Max would probably feel right at home here. Her room had furnishings that belonged in a palace—heavy velvet draperies, plush emerald carpeting, and a spectacular view of Lake Michigan.

Briefly, she thought of her Detroit cousins, Cole and Zack Bailey, who'd each recently fallen in love and gotten married. She was close in proximity but decided not to call them. She had enough on her plate.

It was already late afternoon, and she'd be in a real fix if the bag didn't turn up immediately. Max was escorting her to a benefit for his grandfather's favorite charity, and this was The Night. Once he used the M-word, as in marry, every paper in the country would want pictures of the woman who was going to be the prince's bride. She had to have that bag.

While she waited, she decided she'd better check in with her editor before he went home for the weekend. In Miami it was already after five, so she put through the call. "Waverly, it's Bailey."

"'Bout time you checked in. Where are you?"

"Chicago."

"I'm going to have a hell of a time with accounting when you turn in your expenses."

"Actually, this isn't costing the magazine anything." She felt awkward making the admission.

"We're paying your salary, so it's still costing. What about this thing you have with the prince?"

"I told you it's only a business arrangement. He asked me to pose as his fiancée to discourage the throng of admirers—princess wannabes. Before he leaves, I get an exclusive. He'll answer anything I ask."

"Sounds okay." That was hearty approval, Waverly-style. "How are you going to handle the breakup?"

"He's going to let me dump him."

Ed Waverly laughed so loudly she held the phone away from her ear. It wasn't *that* funny.

"I like the angle—inside story by the woman who scorned Prince Max."

"No, I'm going to do a piece I can be proud of—what it really means to be royalty in the twenty-first century."

"Write a thesis on it if you like, but give me a story that will sell magazines. Remember who signs your paycheck."

Yeah, yeah, yeah, she wanted to say, but her editor's tolerance for sass was low.

"I know my job," she reminded him mildly.

"Keep in touch."

The phone went dead in her ear.

"You have a nice weekend, too," she grumbled, but it was the missing bag that was really bugging her. She was used to her boss' lack of phone manners.

She closed her eyes and tried to concentrate on the chain of events. The first-class seats on the plane had been so comfortable she'd slept most of the way from New York, where Max had spent the day conferring with a banking consortium. She'd enjoyed an afternoon at the Guggenheim Museum, then gone to dinner at a French restaurant with Hans, who'd been relieved of his prince-watching duties to escort her.

Conversation had consisted mainly of a continuation of his lecture on Schwanstein; she'd half expected to be quizzed when he finished. He had shyly answered a few personal questions, telling her he had a fiancée who worked at the post office...

Her mind was wandering. Think! She had to concentrate on their arrival at the hotel. Max's men had handled everything, even though she was reluctant to let the duffel carrying the camera and recorder out of her sight. Max had assured her it was completely safe in their care. He was right—it was sitting on the dresser. But where the heck was the evening gown bag?

Relying on men was always a mistake. She called the desk in the lobby and reported the missing bag.

"I need it right away," she added.

Checking in at the hotel had gone smoothly with Albert in charge. She almost felt guilty for insisting she could choose her own outfits and order her own room service.

Max had been aloof; in fact, he'd hardly talked to her since they'd gotten back from the private beach in Florida. He gave the impression he was single-handedly running his principality, even burying his nose in papers on the plane.

The flight, check-in... Wait a minute. Was she so dazzled by the royal procession she was getting dense? By some strange coincidence—or scheming contrivance—Natasha had shown up in the lobby just when they'd arrived.

"What a wonderful coincidence," she'd trilled to Max.

"Think, think, think," Leigh told herself.

She'd seen something—just a fleeting glimpse buried somewhere in her subconscious.

"That's it!"

Natasha had seemed to be leaving the hotel when she'd cornered Max, but on the way to the elevator Leigh had seen the back of a very tall raven-haired woman carrying a black bag.

Guests didn't carry bags at the Jefferson Arms. And how many women in the entire city of Chicago were six foot two and wore heels?

"That supermodel from hell stole my gowns!" Leigh was stunned.

But it made sense. If Cinderella couldn't go to the ball, the ugly stepsister might have a chance with the prince.

"In your dreams," Leigh said, quickly dialing the desk to get Natasha's room number. They were reluctant until she said the model might have picked up the missing garment bag by mistake. Mentioning the prince probably tipped the scale.

Leigh tried phoning her, but there was no answer. She left her room and raced to the elevator but didn't have any success when she got to Natasha's room.

She had a premonition: she'd see Natasha again

before the evening was over. The real question was, did Max invite her to come to Chicago? Maybe she wasn't one of the women he was trying to avoid.

Leigh had once spent seven hours watching cars race around and around a track with a date who kept belching from all the bratwurst sausages he ate. She'd rather do that again than go to her faux engagement party with no dress and Natasha hovering around Max.

Not that she had any interest in Max's love life. It was no concern of hers if he liked a woman with the soul of a cash register. Interviewing Natasha—real name, Debbie Krump—had been a yawn. She should have gotten an award for fiction writer of the year for making the model sound like a human being.

Being mad didn't solve her problem. When did stores close in Chicago? She started down to the lobby, then realized she didn't have her purse. By the time she got back to her room, the whole thing seemed hopeless.

Even if she could find a classy store open after five, she'd have to mortgage her future to buy a dress like the ones Max had bought.

She called the desk again, this time working her way up to an assistant manager. He apologized profusely, but the bag was still missing.

A half hour before she had to leave, she called the

desk again. The night manager was on duty now. She explained all over again, even though she was pretty sure he'd heard all about the hysterical woman who'd lost her luggage.

It was no use; she'd have to call off the engagement.

But then she might never see Max again.

What did she know about the royal wrath? She'd seen him annoyed, but his sense of humor seemed to put the brakes on his temper. That didn't mean he wouldn't call off their deal if she was a no-show.

"This is ridiculous!" She had two suitcases full of new clothes. There had to be something she could wear.

She laid all the possibilities out on the bed: suits, a sleeveless cotton dress, even her own rust skirt and top. A suit might pass; people wore them everywhere —except formal evening parties.

When the dreaded tap came on the door, she was still darting around the bed in her panty hose and bra, trying to decide which outfit would be the lesser evil.

She ran to the door and shouted through it, "I'm nearly ready."

Ready to die! Max was expecting the spa-perfect woman he'd taken to the Braeworthys' party in Florida. She'd abandoned all attempts at recreating the upswept do, letting her hair hang loose and straight, and she'd been too agitated to do more with her face than her usual mascara and lipstick.

She looked at the choices spread out on the bed. It would have to be the black suit. She yanked the skirt over her head and worked it over her hips. It was snug and short, perfect with the jacket, but no one wore a dinner suit to a black tie affair.

She didn't need X-ray eyes to see Max and his entourage waiting impatiently on the other side of the door. On impulse she grabbed a sleeveless white satin shell still lying in the suitcase. She couldn't even remember buying it, but she slipped it over her head and quickly found her own gold locket. The blouse was made to hang loose, barely touching the waistband of the skirt. It was a go; it had to be. She opened the door.

"Good evening." Max was standing there alone, his bodyguards hovering near the elevator door down the hall. "You look lovely."

His compliment sounded spontaneous and heartfelt, but he was so darned polite, how could she be sure?

"I'm sorry I'm not wearing an evening gown. My bag was stolen—at least, it's missing."

"How fortuitous. I can't imagine a gown that would make you more beautiful than you are now. Simplicity suits you."

"You look very nice, too," she said. It was easily the understatement of her life. The man was born to wear a tuxedo. The black satin cummerbund called attention to his slim waist in contrast to his broad chest covered by the gleaming white pleats of his shirt. She embarrassed herself by staring a moment too long.

They took the limo, Albert in front beside the driver, and Hans and the other bodyguard, Fred, sitting on jump seats facing them.

"I hope you'll enjoy my grandfather's museum," Max said in the same tone Hans used for his Schwanstein lectures.

"The Goth Museum of Functional Art," she said, remembering the name the meatpacker baron had given the museum he'd endowed. "I'm not quite sure what to expect."

"His hobby was collecting what's sometimes called industrial art—objects manufactured from the late 1800s through the 1940s. Some are actually beautiful."

He looked directly at her; she could almost imagine he was thinking about her, not the collection. "I'll let you be surprised. You're always surprising me."

Her skirt was made for standing; this was the first time she'd sat in it, and she didn't dare cross her legs or move the small silver evening purse off her lap. She'd goofed on that, as well. It was too dressy for her outfit and didn't go with her yellow-gold locket.

She felt like squirming, but three pairs of eyes kept her pinned to the spot. She'd give a month's salary to see herself as Max was seeing her. He was too polite to even hint she'd be as out of place as a bag lady at a fashion show.

"I know your mother was Madeline Goth, but how did the daughter of a Chicago meatpacker come to marry your father?"

"She very nearly didn't. My aunt, her older sister, was hosting a party and insisted she come. Aunt Ruthie was notorious for her matchmaking antics, so my mother absolutely refused to agree to be there. Then she met my father at the home of a family friend. He was their houseguest, and he was so taken with her he persuaded her to let him escort her to a party that evening."

"Let me guess! He took her to her own sister's party."

"You guessed it."

"What a wonderful story."

"I used to tease her that their meeting was a fairy tale come true. She never denied it. Ah, here we are."

Whatever she'd expected, it wasn't this hulking

brick building. It looked more like a place for a hockey game than a posh party.

"The outside doesn't look like much, but my grandfather was instrumental in having it placed on the historical register. It was built shortly after the great fire—the one supposedly started by a cow kicking over a lantern."

"That would be Mrs. O'Leary's cow." She wasn't about to tell him she had O'Leary cousins. Her genealogy wasn't quite on a par with his.

"It started as a corset factory, then became the liveliest brothel in the city during the 1920s, according to my grandfather. It housed a speakeasy when liquor was illegal and later several other businesses. He bought it to use as a warehouse and had it totally renovated before his death." Another history lesson, she thought, a little disappointed because Max was being so polite—not that there was anything wrong with good manners.

She loved his, but he could be talking to a tour group from Dubuque. She wanted to know important things. Did he hate her outfit? Was he planning to kiss her again?

Their reception inside the building was superbly orchestrated, with the museum director and several wealthy patrons doing the honors. Everyone adored

Max, even those who were meeting him for the first time.

Was it gratitude for his grandfather's generosity— or did they appreciate the fact that the prince stayed in his little principality most of the time and let them run things?

Or maybe it was the royal mystique in action again. Whatever the reason, they loved him.

She was having a pretty good time, all things considered. Who would have guessed toasters and vacuum cleaners could be fascinating? All she ever did with her household appliances was burn toast and sweep floors.

Max was talking to a silver-haired couple when Leigh saw Natasha hovering near a display of meat-slicing equipment. She looked like a stalk of celery towering over her tubby little escort. To Leigh's immense satisfaction, she was wearing a long gown in chartreuse, the color Max hated.

As the guest of honor, Max had to be first at a buffet table the length of a city block. Because there were so many guests at the five-hundred-dollar-a-plate benefit, the sponsors had opted for a casual arrangement of round tables, closely packed in the large reception room.

It was after nine o'clock, and hungry men and women hovered in the vicinity of the food, waiting to descend on salmon molded into fish shapes, immense mounds of beef and ham, huge bowls heaped high with salads, and platters of other goodies. Max chose this moment of great gastronomic anticipation for his announcement.

"Ladies and gentlemen, friends," he said in a resonant voice that commanded attention, "I'm greatly honored to be with you tonight. Of all my grandfather's accomplishments, none brought him more pleasure than assembling this collection for the Goth Museum of Functional Art. Because of the great affection I had for him, I've chosen this reception to make a very important announcement. I'd like to present to you Miss Leigh Bailey of Florida. Some of you may know of her as a writer for *Celebrity* magazine."

He inclined his head toward the photographers clustered off to the right where they wouldn't hold up the stampede to the food.

"Miss Bailey has done me the honor of consenting to be my bride."

She knew it was coming, but there was no way a girl could prepare for a taste of paradise. Max put his arms around her and bent his head. She should have shut her eyes, but she was mesmerized by his dark spiky lashes and warm brown eyes.

Then he kissed her. She saw his closed lids, beautiful under sharply defined eyebrows. Her own lids dropped, creating a darkness that concentrated her whole being on the lips gently moving against hers.

It was a long kiss, but a sensation like this could never last too long.

Not until he released her did she notice the excited buzzing of voices or the lightning-bug effect of camera flashes.

Now she was supposed to walk the length of the table and fill a plate with princess-size portions. Max handed her a gold-rimmed china plate and motioned her forward.

How did potential princesses eat? She didn't know whether to take tiny dibs and dabs of a few things or heap her plate in appreciation of the sumptuous feast. How could she possibly use lips blessed by a prince's kiss for something as mundane as eating?

More to the point, was her skirt too tight for a big meal?

"You're scarcely taking anything," Max said when they reached the midway point at the table.

She looked down and saw an olive and a smear of something green.

"I'm saving room for"—she quickly glanced ahead to see what was there—"carrot salad. I love carrots and raisins."

At the end of the table he wasn't satisfied that she had her fill.

"Here, allow me." He took her plate and held it out to the chef carving a generous portion of juicy pink roast beef.

With his help, she managed to escape a barrage of congratulations from all sides and reach the table reserved for them. Slumping down on a chair and concealing half of herself under a long linen tablecloth gave her some perspective on the situation.

"For a minute there I must have gotten stage fright," she candidly admitted to him.

"I'm the only one who noticed." He smiled, and she felt surrounded by the glow of a thousand candles.

"Thank you," she murmured.

"Whatever for?" He didn't take his eyes off her.

She shrugged. "For being so nice."

That didn't begin to tell him how she felt, but others were joining them. He squeezed her hand under the table and went back to being the prince.

She couldn't eat. She tried, but food seemed to stick in her throat. People included her in the conversation. She heard herself answering—sometimes she was actually witty—but her real self felt detached from the small talk around her.

She knew what was wrong with her. It was the

bane of her existence not being able to fool herself. This was one big phony act, and she wanted it to be real.

Max rested his hand on her thigh for a moment, and she brushed it away. It hurt to be caressed when she was only a temporary convenience.

Suddenly, she had to get away from this circle of tuxedoed heads and bejeweled bosoms. She couldn't stand to hear another inane question about the glorious principality of Schwanstein. She needed to touch base with reality.

"Will you excuse me, please?" she said to the table in general.

Max stood as she rose to leave, and several other men followed his example.

"I'll be right back," she lied, hurrying away as fast as decorum and her tight skirt allowed.

She needed a strong dose of gritty realism, and she knew where to get it. Guided by her strong survival instinct, not her faulty sense of direction, she found the public-entry area with a phone on the desk behind the counter.

She didn't have room for her cell phone in the dinky little evening bag, but Waverly would think a collect call from her had to be important. Like any good reporter, she knew her editor's phone number by heart.

"What's up?" he asked after agreeing to accept the charge.

"I'm engaged."

"Congratulations."

"Don't take it seriously. It's only a business arrangement."

"I knew that already. You've told me repeatedly." To his credit, he didn't mention that he was paying for the call. "So what's up?"

"I'm just keeping you informed. Could you do me one small favor? I'd like to take a week's vacation starting now."

"Why?"

Why? She didn't know. It just didn't feel right to be working for the magazine—and for Max. She had to face facts. This magical interlude was a charade. She had a vague hope that doing it on her own time might make her less uncomfortable.

"I won't have time to do any writing. It just seems fair."

"You've got it."

"I'll call you after my vacation," she promised.

Until Leigh left the table, Max had been having a

marvelous time. Now the chitchat seemed stifling; he was too restless to sit still another moment.

"If you'll excuse me, ladies and gentlemen, I believe I'll see what's keeping Miss Bailey—my fiancée."

He had no intention of checking the ladies' room. He had a hunch she wasn't there. Acting on some instinct he didn't want to examine, he started toward the main entrance. Fortunately, he heard her voice before she saw him. He had no right to spy on her, but he heard her mention being engaged. She had to be talking to someone connected with her magazine.

What had he expected from her? That she play the blushing bride-to-be and ignore the news value of his announcement?

He left before she saw him, angry at her for rushing to the phone to report her news immediately. He was even angrier at himself for getting mixed up in such a ridiculous situation. She was beautiful, but so were lots of women. He knew better than to get involved with a reporter. What had he been thinking?

He steeled himself to return to his duties. Most of what he did as prince was playacting, but playing the loving fiancé was going to be a stretch after this episode.

He wanted to admonish the conniving little

reporter—or take her to bed. But that was a complication he could not allow to happen.

He clenched his fists, took a deep breath, and returned to the table where the museum director and dignitaries were waiting for him.

She didn't return. At first it was a relief not having to play the doting fiancé while he was angry. But then his anger subsided, and he started to worry. The neighborhood south of the museum had an unsavory reputation. If she decided to leave on her own...

He should have ordered Hans to keep an eye on her. If she went outside to find a taxi at this time of night, anything could happen. He told himself she wasn't foolish; in fact, he'd never met a woman better able to fend for herself. But he was still worried.

"If you'll excuse me, I'm afraid Leigh isn't feeling herself tonight. I should check on her again. It's been a great pleasure." He smiled, shook hands, called people by name. It was his job: the royal dismissal.

He went directly to Hans, who was surveying the milling crowd from a vantage point near the wide entryway on the west side.

"Have you seen Miss Bailey recently?" Max asked.

"Yes, Your Highness. She went up the stairs about ten minutes ago."

"She was fascinated by the kitchen gadgets," Max mumbled, embarrassed admitting, even to one of the men who virtually lived in his pocket, that his fiancée had disappeared on him. "Watch the front entrance. If you see her, tell her I'm looking for her."

He ran up the flight of broad steps built as part of his grandfather's renovations, feeling more winded than the climb warranted. A few people had left the reception area to wander among the displays again, and he was held up by the need to be marginally courteous when they spoke to him.

His stiff-necked pride wouldn't allow him to ask anxious questions or run about calling her name. The converted warehouse was damnably large, but he managed to determine she was nowhere on the second level.

The third and top floor was devoted to patented failures, a favorite of his grandfather's: peculiar inventions that never quite lived up to their inventors' expectations. He started searching for her in the maze of rooms, struck by the irony of searching for his "fiancée" among things that had disappointed their originators.

Several people were chuckling over a helmet that was supposed to stimulate hair growth with mild electrical shocks. Rogaine it wasn't. Max managed to avoid them, growing more worried as he eliminated places where she could be. And warmer. It was unseasonably hot for September—or so people repeatedly told him—and there was no air-conditioning system on this level. He went into a room full of farm-related devices, surprised to see that a small door leading to a fire escape had been left open.

A faint but welcome whiff of cooler air drew him closer, then prompted him to step outside onto the iron grating. "Leigh, what are you doing out here?"

Her face was a pale oval framed by silky hair, and he forgot his anger.

"I'm just getting some air."

"I think you're hiding. I searched every room on two floors looking for you."

"I should have gone back to the table. My job for the evening wasn't quite done, was it?"

"No doubt you had a good reason for staying away." He was inviting her to explain her absence; she didn't.

"I'm sorry about the way I'm dressed. My bag of evening gowns really was stolen after we got to the hotel."

"I'll have Albert check in the morning. He's very good at finding lost things, but you have nothing to apologize for. You're beautiful just the way you are." He reached out and fingered her locket, wishing he had the right to open it.

"You're being kind."

"No, I mean it." He took a deep breath, amazed

because she genuinely didn't realize how lovely she was. "What you're wearing is perfect. Every man in the room envied me tonight."

She laughed softly, but he could hear a haunting sadness in the sound. Or was he imagining depth that didn't exist? He'd never been less sure of anyone.

"Is there something you want me to do?" she asked.

He wanted her to explain away the phone call she'd made, but he couldn't ask her about it without admitting he'd hung back in the shadows and eaves-dropped. Why couldn't he have run a nurse or a teacher off the road? Why did she have to be a journalist?

"You've played your part well. I won't ask more of you this evening," he said.

She turned away from him, looking down on a well-lit parking area and a pair of dumpsters. He didn't want to leave her there alone.

"What do you think of my grandfather's muse-um?" he asked.

"It's interesting. I never dreamed machines could have so much style, so much soul. I love the outboard motor that looks like part of an airplane."

"It wasn't very successful on boats, I'm afraid."

"I guess a lot of things that look wonderful don't live up to expectations."

The sadness was back in her voice; he drew closer, feeling big and clumsy beside her finely molded shoulders and slender bare arms. He reached out with his knuckles, rubbing them against the thin satin covering one of her shoulder blades.

"Leigh."

She turned and faced him, backed against the steel railing of the landing, so close her perfume teased his nostrils.

"You really do look"—he groped for words —"stunning."

He wanted to kiss her, really kiss her, without the restraint of being watched. He knew the outline of her lips and the sweetness of her mouth, but he wanted to know much more. How would she sound in the throes of passion? Was she daring enough to trust him completely?

He leaned forward, putting his hands on the rail to imprison her between his arms. Everything was against this—fair play, common sense, and his own promise not to take advantage of their arrangement. She started to say something, but the words didn't come. He covered her mouth with his and wrapped his arms around her.

She couldn't breathe. No kiss had lasted this long or felt this wonderful. Then his breath was warm on her cheek, and she gasped for air, ready when he drew her lips between his and did magical, wonderful things.

This wasn't a kiss; it was lovemaking. She didn't want to resist. Her hands found the muscular leanness of his rib cage under his jacket and clung to him like a drowning victim.

Light-headed, dizzy with arousal, she let his tongue slide deeper and deeper, fusing her need and his desire.

The faint light coming from the inside of the building went off, then on again, blinking three times.

"Our signal to leave," he whispered huskily.

"Or we'll be locked in?"

"I don't think Albert will allow that to happen."

He was supposed to watch out for the prince, so why wasn't he here to prevent this, she thought, halfway between elation and despair. What was happening here? This wasn't the way business partners kissed each other—not that they should kiss each other at all.

"We have to go." Max sounded stern and determined.

She obeyed, wondering how she could face the elegant strangers after this. She might as well have "I've been making out with the prince" tattooed on her forehead.

"The car will be waiting at the service entrance. Follow me," Max ordered.

She resisted the impulse to stick her tongue out at him. Sure, she'd follow him. All he had to offer was a wildly exciting, totally insane ride on an emotional roller coaster.

## ✣ 6 ✣

He'd lost control last night.

Max was ashamed, but there it was. If he'd had to walk through throngs of people, someone would surely have noticed his...agitation. As it was, he'd had to scowl and send his men scurrying on needless errands while he hurried Leigh into the limo.

Otherwise one of them would have noticed something was amiss. He employed them to be alert and observant. They never disappointed.

He *was* disappointed—in himself. Worse, he felt guilty as sin. He'd given his word of honor, not something he did lightly, even to a woman whose only interest in him was professional.

When he started searching for her in the museum, he'd fully intended to vent his anger on her.

Was she so eager to dissect him in print she had to rush to a phone in the middle of a social engagement?

Then, when he'd finally found her on the fire escape landing...

"Stop here," he said to Albert, who was driving the sedan through still-heavy morning traffic. "You won't be able to park—Just circle until I come out, hopefully in twenty minutes or so."

Like a man about to do penance, he got out of the car and resolutely entered the large department store, hoping sunglasses would cut down on the recognition factor. Hans was behind him, keeping a wary eye out for physical danger, but Max knew he had more to fear from adoration than assault. Americans, deprived by the lack of a royal family, were always designating someone King of Rock and Roll or Crown Prince of Baseball. When real royalty visited, they went wild.

He sighed. It would be nice to travel incognito, but the tabloids guaranteed that was impossible.

Leigh stared at the latest delivery: a huge bouquet of long-stemmed yellow roses. It was squeezed between a fall-color arrangement and the American beauty reds on the windowsill. Who were all these people with a hotline to flower shops? Did they get up at dawn to score social points with the newly engaged prince? Her hotel room looked like a funeral parlor.

She needed to jog or at least take a long, fast walk, but she was totally daunted by the prospect of going through the hotel lobby. She'd never dreamed it was so complicated to be one of the beautiful people. She needed a disguise, and sunglasses alone wouldn't do it. She thought of wearing her rumpled jeans, stuffed into her own bag, and pigtails, but how inconspicuous could she be with Fred following her?

Apparently, he'd lost the toss today; he was her designated shadow.

She flipped TV channels for the hundredth time; it was like biting down on an aching tooth to test how bad it was. Somehow TMZ had found Doug Bolt, Dopey Doug, a boy she'd gone out with once in the tenth grade. Some bimbo in Orlando led him through an interview that ran every half hour after the hippo-birth piece. Dopey called her an angel who kissed like a goddess.

"Jerk!" She couldn't even remember kissing him.

Dopey Doug's interview was due again when someone knocked.

"If it's more flowers, I swear I'll load them all on a housekeeping cart," she muttered, opening the door.

"Hello."

"Oh, it's you."

"May I come in?" Max asked, his arms so full she had to close the door after him.

"If you're not allergic to flowers. Have you seen this?" She gestured at the TV. "I dated that opportunist once when I was fifteen. He makes it sound like I was the love of his life."

"No doubt you were." Max was grinning. "If it's on television, it must be true."

"You're enjoying this. You knew what would happen. Why did you get me into this...this..."

"Circus? Media feeding frenzy? Welcome to my world, Leigh," he said with good-humored irony. "May I put these things on the bed? I don't see any place else."

"You found the garment bag." She took it from him, putting it down to unzip it. "Everything seems to be here."

"Your gown for the Silver and Gold Ball is, fortunately. It appears somebody was pulling a prank. The bag was found inside a locked stall in the ladies' room. The thief went to a great deal of trouble."

"She, or he, crawled under?"

"Had to."

Leigh laughed, enjoying the thought of Natasha slinking under the door on her belly like the snake she was. But she couldn't share her suspicion with

Max. He might think she was making a false accusation because she was jealous of the model.

"How did you get it back?" she asked.

"Albert made it known that the employee who returned it would receive a sizable reward, no questions asked."

He was still holding a big plastic department store bag. She turned off the TV; the sudden silence was awkward.

"I had an opportunity to survey the merchandise in one of your large stores," he said, beginning to doubt the wisdom of his purchase.

"You mean you went shopping? Every tourist should give it a whirl, I guess. Did you buy a present for your father?"

"I guess I'm a bad son. It didn't even occur to me."

Part of him wanted to tell the truth—that he hadn't thought of anyone but her since he'd found her on the fire escape landing. But how could he admit that to a woman who was counting the hours until she could interrogate him for her story?

"Well, thank you for bringing the garment bag," she said.

"You're welcome. Are your accommodations satis-factory?"

"Yes, fine. Is there some protocol about flowers? Should I write thank-you notes? I've never heard of most of the senders."

"I'll have Albert take care of it. Just give him the signature cards with a notation of what was sent, if you would, please."

"Could he do something with the flowers? Maybe send them to a nursing home? It seems wasteful to have so many here. But the roses are beautiful, aren't they?"

"Stunning."

He didn't mean the flowers. She seemed to give off a glow, a radiance that enchanted him in spite of the devil's bargain he'd struck with her. He couldn't blame her for their situation. It had made sense at the time to ask her to pose as his fiancée. He should have foreseen the complications, but holding her in his arms while the hurricane threatened had dulled his reasoning powers.

"This is for you," he said.

He held out the bag.

She didn't take it.

He laid it on the bed. "Please, open it and see if you like it."

"Is this something you want me to wear?"

He sensed her reluctance and tried to explain.

"Only if you choose to. It's a gift for you—not part of the wardrobe you insist be donated to a charitable cause."

"A souvenir of our brief engagement?"

"An apology."

She looked up sharply, still hanging back as though she expected something in the box to bite her. He'd never had such a hard time presenting a gift to a woman.

"I promised not to take advantage of our arrangement. I broke my word last evening," he said. "I had no right to kiss you."

"About that—"

"Open your gift."

He watched intently as she lifted the cover of the box and folded back the tissue.

"What is it?"

"Take it out."

She unfurled the midnight blue velvet and touched the glittering rhinestone clip.

"It's a cape." She sounded astonished.

"You'll need an evening wrap. Let me help you."

He took the soft satin-lined velvet and draped it around her shoulders, letting his hands linger for a moment on the incredibly soft fabric. "Do you like it?"

"It's beautiful! I love it. You'll have to take it back. Don't laugh! I mean it, Max."

"That's why I'm laughing—you *do* mean it. Will your journalistic integrity be compromised if you accept my small gift as an apology?"

What a gift she had—for making him angry and amused at the same time. Unfortunately, nothing she did diminished his desire for her.

"About last night—it can't happen again," she said, not meeting his eyes.

"It?"

"You know what I mean."

He shook his head, refusing to make it easy for her.

"Please, don't kiss me again. It's not part of our deal."

"Yes, I overstepped the boundaries of our agreement. This is my peace offering. I'll be grateful if you accept it." He held his hands out, palms up, wondering why it was so important to him.

"As long as you understand." She lifted a fold of the velvet and ran it over her inner wrist. "I've never felt anything so soft. Thank you, Max. It's the loveliest thing I've ever worn."

He wanted to wrap it around her naked body and make love to her in the midst of its folds, but those thoughts would drive him crazy.

"I'm here to take you somewhere," he said, forcing himself to concentrate on more mundane matters.

"Should I change?" She took off the cape and carefully refolded it in the box. "It's so complicated knowing what to wear when I'm with you. Maybe I should have Albert advise me."

"Your instincts are marvelous. Wear what pleases you. But you're fine dressed the way you are."

"But I'm wearing my own clothes." She stared down at the rust-colored skirt and ballet flats.

"Don't worry. We have a long drive, and we're expected for tea."

"Tea?"

"Come on." He grabbed her hand.

Max escorted her through the lobby and into the front seat of the waiting sedan.

"No bodyguards?" she asked, clicking on her seat belt.

"None needed."

"Where are we going?"

"On a mystery trip."

"Tell me. I don't like surprises."

"Curiosity or caution?" he teased.

"I like to know where I'm going."

"You will in due time."

"Max! Don't do this to me."

He pulled out into traffic, seemingly at ease in the city's congestion.

"Do you need GPS?" She opened the map app on her phone.

"Chicago is my second home. I've been coming here since I was a boy. Darcy and I used to play together like brother and sister. Her mother is from here."

"Are we going to see her?"

"Good Lord, no! She travels with the jet set—or so she likes to think. Her husband is writing a book on casino gambling. He's been researching it for twenty-some years."

"You sound disapproving. Don't you like to gamble?"

"I don't like to lose." He glanced at her and smiled. "And all gamblers do lose eventually. I'd rather buy gifts for beautiful women."

"No doubt you expect a payoff of another kind," she said dryly.

"Playboy prince scores again? I almost believe you're addicted to the tabloids, Leigh."

"I'm not."

He was baiting her, and she'd jumped right into the trap. "Then what proof do you have I'm a womanizer?" he asked.

"You just said—"

"Hearsay."

"Not when it comes from the subject."

"Still not proof. If I told you I was secretly married to Meghan Markle, and she was a bigamist, would you rush to print it?"

"Of course not. I'd check other sources for confirmation."

"Knowing it could be a fabrication?"

"It is, isn't it?"

"See, I've proved my case. You want to believe sensationalist garbage."

"That's not true." She stared out the window, only dimly aware he was entering an expressway. He was exasperating, and she wished she hadn't come.

"How much longer will this charade last?" she asked crossly.

"You'll be pleased with the brevity of our engagement."

"Do you ever give a straight answer? If you weren't a prince, you'd probably be a politician."

"I'm flattered you think I'm not one."

"Royalty doesn't have to run for office."

"No, but free people have the right to abolish their monarchy."

"You can be voted out of your job?"

"Of course, although the possibility is remote. In fact, there's a worse danger. If I fail to produce an heir, the Principality of Schwanstein will be annexed to Austria on my death."

"While we're on the subject, aren't you driving too fast?" She glanced at the speedometer. "Or are you trying to read the bumper sticker on that pickup?"

"If you're asking whether I learned my lesson, I did."

"Where are we going, Max?"

**"Prince Abducts Reporter?"**

"I'm a writer, a magazine writer. There's a difference." He swerved abruptly from the middle to the left lane and sped past a red van. "And you're not a race-car driver!"

"Are you asking me to slow down?"

"Yes! Please!"

He immediately fell into line behind a white compact with no bumper sticker.

"Is this better?"

He was steering with one hand, his driving style bordering on recklessness even at the lower speed.

"Yes, thank you, but I'd feel better if you used two hands."

"Your wish is my command."

"Then tell me where we're going."

"To see my great-aunt Lucinda, the last of the Goths, my grandfather's sister. She was ninety last

May, and her tongue is as sharp as a chopping knife, so be warned. She has an uncanny gift for taking people apart to see what makes them tick. She never liked my father."

"Why not?"

"She loathed the Duke and Duchess of Windsor —no one is quite sure why. Maybe they slighted her in some way back when she was a debutante. Whatever the reason, she's a virulent royal basher."

"She didn't approve of your mother's marriage?"

"No. Mother was her favorite. She wanted her to be the wife of a president—or at least a senator."

"But she never married herself."

"You're sure you don't know about Lucinda?" He slowed for a tollbooth. "I forgot about these blasted things. Do you have fifty cents in coins?"

"It's the least I can do," she said dryly, digging into the bottom of her purse for some loose change and handing it to him. "What about Lucinda?"

He tossed the coins into the hopper and waited a moment for the green light to flash.

"The great love of her life was a president."

"She had…"

"An affair, yes."

"I've never heard of her."

"Things were done more discreetly in her day."

"Which president? How…?"

"It's her secret, Leigh. Please respect her privacy in your article."

"Whatever you think about me, I wouldn't stoop that low by repeating old rumors."

"There weren't any rumors. I'm just explaining why she didn't think the Prince of Schwanstein was suitable for her favorite niece. She gloried in real power."

Leigh expected a grandiose old mansion or an exclusive resident hotel. Instead, their long trip ended at an impressive but not overly large 1920s Tudor-style home with frontage on Lake Michigan. She wasn't even sure whether they were in Illinois or Wisconsin, and Max had lapsed into a brooding silence.

"Is she expecting us?" Leigh asked when they drove through the open gateway of an ornate cast-iron fence.

"She'd probably slap my wrist with her fan if I didn't call first."

"Is she really such a terror? If you're trying to make me nervous, you've succeeded."

"You'll have to judge for yourself. She'll have heard the news," he said, stopping the car in a circular drive in front of a brick and half-timbered house. "We'll see if you pass muster."

"Max, this wasn't part of our deal! Aren't you going to tell her the truth?"

"I'll let you make that decision."

He went up a tier of circular steps, leaving her to follow, and pressed a chime that reverberated through the dark paneled door.

The uniformed woman who opened it was as tall as Max and had beefy arms almost as thick as her neck and iron-gray hair braided on top of her head.

"Your Highness," she said in heavily accented English. "So good you've come to see her. Ach, she's been impossible since you called. So many orders. So much fuss."

"Leigh, this is Miss Schmidt. She's been with my aunt for how long—forty years, forty-five?"

"*Ja*, you're close. Forty-seven come next April."

Leigh followed Max through an art-deco time warp to a rear sitting room with white wicker furnishings and a big bay window.

"Aunt Lucinda."

Max hurried forward and kissed the proffered cheek of a tall slender woman in severe brown trousers and an ivory turtleneck sweater. Her hair was white and piled haphazardly on top of her head, strands falling onto the sides of her wrinkled cheeks. Her sapphire-blue eyes apparently hadn't faded with age.

"So, this is your fiancée." She took Leigh's hand and squeezed it with surprising firmness. "You don't look anything like that Wallis Simpson woman. That's good. I can't abide the vampire look, all black hair and red lips. Only a congenital idiot like Eddie would want to climb into bed with her."

"Aunt Lucinda—"

"Oh, now, you keep still, Max. I don't leave the house much anymore, but I know what's going on out there." She gestured dramatically. "Nothing I say is going to shock your young lady."

She picked up a folded ivory fan and opened it with a flourish, fanning herself for an instant, then snapping it shut and shaking it at Max.

"I warned your father—an heir and a spare. It's the only thing the Brits do right. Imagine if they'd had to depend on Eddie." She wagged the fan at Leigh. "I hope you have a bun in the oven. These things shouldn't be left to chance." She wagged the fan at Leigh.

"No," Leigh said emphatically before Max could answer. "And frankly, Miss Goth, it's not your concern."

She watched Lucinda clutch the closed fan and drum it on the arm of a wicker chair, expecting to have her knuckles whacked for her impudence.

Instead, the old woman laughed hoarsely, her whole face wrinkling with glee.

"I like your fiancée, Max. She has spunk—or whatever you call it today when a female speaks her mind. You and your father, both so handsome and so popular with the girls. I warned your mother—it's no picnic to be involved with royalty. Have you thought about the ramifications, young lady?"

"Leigh. My name is Leigh Bailey."

"Ah, an Irish name. That explains it. Max, I have something for you, a portrait of your mother taken by my dear friend, Howard Styles. It's in a silver frame in the green bedroom. Go fetch it, dear, while Leigh and I talk girl talk. Now don't look sullen. Just run along."

Max smiled indulgently, winked at Leigh, and left her alone with the dragon lady.

Later they had tea—cucumber sandwiches, cherry and lemon tarts, and scalding hot brew served in handleless Chinese cups.

"I don't go to weddings," Lucinda said when they were getting ready to leave. "I was a bridesmaid thirty-seven times, and what a bore it was every time. But if you decide to marry him, you're to have my diamond tiara, my dear."

"I couldn't—"

"We have to leave, Aunt Lucinda," Max said.

"Run along, run along. Leigh will join you in a moment."

When Max was out of hearing, the old woman smiled slyly, leaned close, and told Leigh one more thing.

On the way home Leigh was gratified to learn Max was as curious about things as he accused her of being.

"So you really enjoyed your talk with Aunt Lucinda?" he asked as they neared the city. "She doesn't usually take to people the way she did to you."

"Oh, yes, she's a delight, and she adores you." Leigh knew he wasn't satisfied with the sketchy summary she'd given him of her conversation alone with the old woman. Served him right for being so mysterious about their destination.

"If so, she's an expert at concealing it."

"Because she barks orders and sends you to fetch things?"

"She's eccentric. I'm fond of her, so I indulge her. What was the secret she told you before we left? You didn't tell her about our arrangement, did you?"

"No, it would have spoiled her fun."

"Then what was so secretive?"

"That, Your Highness," she said firmly, "is just between us girls."

Lucinda had been engaging and surprising, jumping from the past to the present with the agility of a kick boxer, but she had to be mistaken about Max. After she'd shooed him out, his great-aunt had insisted he was besotted with his fiancée.

But Leigh wasn't really his fiancée, and she knew better than to listen to an old woman who still believed in fairy-tale romance.

## 7

**M**ax was annoyed.

He was an expert at concealing it, but Leigh saw the way his right eyebrow rose slightly higher than his left, unintentionally revealing his skepticism about what Randolph Davies, the chairman of the board of the Chicago Children's Hospital, was saying.

"Surely the best nursing care isn't a frill, is it?" Max asked as his entourage followed the pompous pencil-thin man onto the Staff Only elevator.

The hospital was a major recipient of funds from the Goth Foundation, established by Max's grandfather. One of Max's responsibilities was to review the foundation's grants.

"CCH is on the cutting edge of new technologies," Davies went on, ignoring the prince's question as the doors slid open on the fifth floor.

Leigh looked at Max and nearly laughed out loud at his pained restraint. He was not pleased, although she was probably the only one who saw his eyes narrow. He started to drum his fingers on his left palm, then instantly checked himself.

Poor Max, she thought, smiling at how odd it was to feel sorry for a man with his advantages. Still, it had to be frustrating listening to a self-serving man like Davies without the option of putting him in his place. The hospital's PR person, a sharp-faced woman with tight auburn curls, had taken notes throughout the luncheon in the hospital's private dining room. She kept on scribbling during the long tour of the facilities.

Except for a few politely reserved words when they were introduced, Max said nothing to the woman directly, but Leigh realized how tedious it was for him to be under such close scrutiny. Did he feel the same way about her presence, knowing she might write about anything he did? She wished they could forget their deal and just be friends. Fat chance.

Davies droned on, oblivious to his royal guest's dissatisfaction, but Leigh was fascinated by Max's public persona. He stopped often to exchange a few words with hospital staff, learning more by asking his own questions than Davies had any intention of telling him.

He loved talking to the children, going into several rooms where the occupants were wide-eyed, resisting their naps. Davies waited in the hallway, frown lines creasing his forehead while Max visited a wan-faced little girl who seemed too small for her hospital bed. He bent down and whispered something in her ear, leaving her with a contented smile.

"I'm glad you asked me to come," Leigh said when the tour finally ended and Hans had been dispatched to bring the sedan up to the main entrance. "It must be wonderful to be involved with something so worthwhile."

"My role is minimal. The foundation has a very hardworking board and a dedicated director. I wish there was more I could do."

"There's the ball. Albert said the cream of Chicago society will be there to meet you—and donate money to the CCH."

"Albert gossips like an old woman," Max said with good humor.

"Women don't have a monopoly on gossip. It's the men in our office who wear out the carpet in front of the coffee machine pontificating over rumors."

"And today women own athletic franchises and run corporations. I stand corrected, Ms. Bailey." He sounded stern, but laugh lines at the corners of his eyes betrayed him.

"You look tired. Will you have time for a nap before the ball?" she asked.

"A nap?" He made the princely harrumph sound. "I have a conference call with a California firm at four, then I'll tackle the day's business."

"I concede. You're busy. You're important. You don't have to make that noise at me."

"What noise?" He frowned.

"Harrumph." She tried to imitate it but ended up giggling.

"Harrumph? Do I do that?"

"Whenever you look down your royal nose at me."

"If I do it again, I'll sentence myself to the dungeons." He smiled broadly, and her heart did wild little flip-flops, reminding her that this gorgeous man was her fiancé—at least temporarily.

"Does Schwanstein have dungeons?" She gave a mock shudder.

"Certainly, in the old castle. I was forbidden to play in them as a boy, which made them the object of more than one secret expedition with my friends."

"I have a hard time imagining you as a boy."

"I was a rascal—in disgrace as often as not. And

unlike my early predecessors, I didn't have a whipping boy."

"A whipping boy?"

"Someone to take my punishment for me. Being a prince isn't what it once was."

"It suits you, though."

He was standing so close the brisk fall breeze didn't carry away the spicy tang of his aftershave. "In what way?"

"Here's the car," she said, saved from answering an unanswerable question.

At the hotel she had time for a short nap before her appointment with the stylist, who was coming to the room to do her hair and makeup for the ball. But she couldn't lie still.

She was alternately excited and scared. The Silver and Gold Ball was the most elegant and prestigious event of the Chicago social scene, and this year was supposed to top anything on the East or West Coast. Hopefully it would also raise a bundle for the CCH, especially with Prince Max there to call attention to the needs of sick children.

The stylist, elegant herself with blunt-cut platinum hair and a burgundy smock, arrived exactly on time, and Leigh whispered thanks to Albert under her breath. She'd have to find a way to thank him for all his help, and she doubted a year's subscription to *Celebrity* would fit the bill.

The stylist stayed to help her with the silver evening gown. The strapless bodice left her shoulders bare while subtle underwiring pushed up her breasts and shaped them into lush mounds. She wiggled, bent, and stretched when her helper wasn't looking, finally satisfied her nipples wouldn't pop out of the daring top.

The clinging floor-length skirt had a short train in back controlled by a silver ribbon tied to her left wrist. She only had to bend her elbow to avoid stepping on it when she turned. In spite of the complicated design, the gown was the ultimate in elegant simplicity. It shimmered like liquid silver and made Leigh feel like a real princess.

The shoes didn't make her so happy. The slender inch-and-a-half heels were designed for dancing, but one slim strap across her toes was all that held them on.

At the last minute the stylist draped the midnight blue cape around her shoulders and refused the tip Leigh offered.

"The prince took care of everything," she said. "You're a very fortunate woman."

Hans came to escort her down to the limo where Max was waiting, standing beside the rear door. He smiled warmly when he saw her, and his face told her even more than words could.

"You're absolutely beautiful," he said for her ears only as he helped her into the car.

Fred and Hans stationed themselves on the jump seats. The romantic moment only lasted an instant, not even enough time to feast her eyes on how wonderful Max looked.

The ball was black tie, with women required to wear gold or silver evening gowns. Max complemented her gown by wearing heavy silver cufflinks shaped like the heads of the mythical beasts on the Schwanstein crest.

They'd ridden only a few blocks when he reached over and took one of her gloved hands in his, sliding his little finger between the tiny buttons to caress her wrist. Streetlights illuminated the interior enough for his handholding to be obvious to the bodyguards, but they were as expressionless as the famous stone lions guarding the Chicago Art Institute.

"I wish I could have every dance with you," Max said softly, releasing her hand and leaning so close his words tickled her ear.

He bent and lightly brushed his lips against her throat, then caught one of her dangly rhinestone earrings between his fingers. "These should be diamonds."

"No, they shouldn't. This is all pretend, Max. Real diamonds wouldn't be appropriate."

"Appropriate?" He gave a short harsh laugh. "How many hopes and desires have been impaled on that word?"

"Are you being philosophical?" she asked, trying to tell herself there was no reason to read anything special into his question.

But he'd managed to spoil her mood. This ball wasn't a romantic encounter; he was taking her for show. Probably her real job for him began tonight. She hated even thinking about the crowds of women who would be vying for his attention.

"Women often fault me for being too much of a realist, but I do have my lapses," he said. "We're making one stop before the ball. I'm sorry for the delay, but you needn't come in. I'll be as quick as possible."

She wasn't wearing a watch, but she knew the ball had already begun. Earlier Albert had said something about the first dance, but she wasn't clear whether that meant no one could dance until Max officially began the festivities.

Max's unscheduled stop seemed even odder when the limo driver pulled near the main entrance of the CCH. Apparently, there were royal privileges even at a children's hospital. Hans and the driver got out and lounged near the hood, leaving the limo in the No Parking zone, while Fred followed Max inside.

What was he doing? She imagined everything from punching the board chairman in the nose to donating blood for a suffering child. Whenever she thought she knew Max pretty well, he surprised her.

The two men strolled a few yards away and lit cigarettes, paying absolutely no attention to her. The rear door was open, letting in the pleasant evening air.

As quietly as she could, she slid across the seat and stepped out onto the pavement. A few people passed the limo with curious glances. There was enough foot traffic so her bodyguard might not hear her. She hiked up the train of her gown and dashed up the steps and into the hospital.

A pair of young doctors in green cotton scrubs gave her curious glances as she rushed past them, but no one challenged her.

Acting on a hunch, she found the bank of elevators they'd used earlier in the day, hoping to retrace the tour with Max. She exited on five, feeling more conspicuous here than in the lobby. She couldn't think of any excuse, plausible or otherwise, for being there in a silver evening gown and velvet cape.

Luck was with her; no one at the nurses' station

noticed when she hurried down the corridor they'd taken earlier.

Some rooms were dark, but she peeped in the door wherever a light was still showing. It didn't take long to find Max.

He was reading to the little girl he'd whispered to earlier in the day, so intent on the story between colorful covers that he didn't see Leigh. She wanted it to stay that way, so she backed across the corridor. From her vantage point, she saw Max smile and point to a page, rewarded by a laugh from the child.

He'd put the ball on hold and come back to read a bedtime story. Her throat felt tight, and she wanted to rush into the room and take both of them in her arms. But Max would put a bad spin on her curiosity; he might even think she was spying on him for her article.

Rather than let that happen, she reluctantly crept away, then rushed toward the elevators. There were five—three on one side with the staff car and another public one across from them. She stabbed at the call button, but the overhead indicators showed every car either on the ground level or lower. She crossed to the opposite wall and pushed that button, then looked vainly around for a stairway.

One and then another elevator started moving upward, but Leigh wanted to stamp her foot at their slowness. What if someone were bleeding up here? Shouldn't hospitals have fast elevators? A third one started moving upward; whoever heard of elevators traveling in packs?

She was being silly. Max wasn't going to yell at her, but she wanted to get back to the limo before he saw her.

The door to her right slid open, and a woman with big daisies on her hospital smock maneuvered a cart full of complicated equipment out of the car. Leigh caught the door before the two sides slid together, slipping inside just as she saw Max coming toward the elevators.

She leaned on the lobby button all the way down, not that she could override commands from people waiting on the floors below. She just needed to be doing something. The elevator stopped once on the third floor, and an elderly couple shuffled in, blocking the door so she had no choice but to wait for them to get out before her on the ground level.

Out of the corner of her eye, she saw that the car next to hers was on the second floor and still descending as she headed into the lobby. Max was probably in it.

She yanked up her train and ran for it.

It was dark outside, but only in comparison to the bright fluorescents in the reception area. Ahead she had her choice of the broad marble steps or the gently sloped ramp. She flung herself down the steps, praying she wouldn't plunge headfirst and ruin her gown. She looked back to see if Max had come out of the elevator yet—then stumbled and sat down hard.

All she'd hurt was her dignity, but she'd lost a shoe in her haste to get down the steps, too. Heart pounding, she turned and saw dark trousers with a satin strip on the sides of the legs—a tux.

Max was standing above her, the lost shoe in the palm of his hand.

"Cinderella, I presume."

Her cheeks flamed, and she opened her mouth to blurt out an excuse, any excuse, for having been in the hospital: thirst, restroom. No words came out.

Max came down to her level, and she couldn't bring herself to lie. She'd spied on him in a beautiful tender moment, and she didn't want to tarnish it with lame excuses. She braced herself for the worst, then Max went down on one knee in front of her.

She stood, lopsided on one heel, frozen with embarrassment. She didn't want him to think she was a nosy royalty-stalking journalist.

He reached out, letting his fingers rest lightly on the side of her ankle. Slowly, he gripped the back of her heel, gently cupping it as he lifted her foot from the ground. His touch was so steadying she stood on one foot with perfect balance, reaching out to him with her heart but not her hands.

He lingered, sliding his palm under her sole, seemingly reluctant to release it. His fingers locked around her toes, warming flesh cold from contact with the pavement.

Moving in slow motion, he brought the shoe to her foot and slid the strap over it.

She tingled from the tips of her toes to the swell of her calf, and then he rose and stood looking down at her. She felt sure more than kindness had brought him to his knees.

"Your dancing slipper, my lady."

He intended to say something frivolous to dispel the passion smoldering between them, but his mind was clouded by the impact of holding her small delicate foot in his hand. He'd wanted to run his hand upward over her shapely nylon-clad leg and caress the roundness of her calf, the hollow behind her knee, the soft tender flesh where her thighs came together.

Her voice seemed to come from another dimension when she murmured her thanks.

"I saw you reading. It was so sweet of you. Will you forgive me for following you?"

"You're forgiven." He took her gloved hand and brought it to his lips, but he didn't want cloth between his skin and hers. He undid the tiny buttons, feeling awkward but accomplishing his task, and peeled back the pristine white gloves.

He didn't kiss her fingers—it was enough to press his lips against each smooth knuckle. Enough for now.

"The orchestra is waiting for us," he said softly, but for him the music had already begun.

And for Leigh, the evening was already perfect. She was so dazzled by the man beside her she hardly saw the posh Grand Ballroom of the Camelot Hotel. Women in silver and gold, gaudy or elegant as their taste dictated, seemed to float on the arms of their escorts, but Leigh discovered what it meant to have eyes for only one person.

She looked at her hand and realized she'd been given a glittering silver mask. Max slipped his on, then carefully took hers and worked it over her elaborately upswept curls.

"You're the most beautiful woman I've ever seen," he whispered.

For this one golden moment she believed him.

Max made excuses on every side for his tardiness, but no one seemed to mind it. He was besieged by glamorous sophisticated women and their self-confident poised escorts, people who blossomed in his presence with smiles and smooth words.

The orchestra had indeed been waiting for Prince Maximilian and his fiancée to begin the dancing. They were alone in the middle of a huge, highly waxed floor when the conductor gave the signal to begin.

She'd worried for days that she wasn't graceful enough, rhythmic enough, to dance with a prince. She'd learned a few moves in middle school gym classes; everything else she knew about dancing was instinctive, picked up in bits and pieces. She didn't do any steps that had a name.

The orchestra began with a waltz. She closed her eyes and let the music flow through her, then she was in Max's arms, her train held high by the wrist ribbon, whirling in perfect harmony with the music.

With his strong hand on her waist, she couldn't misstep. They flowed across the floor, and she didn't even notice when other couples joined them.

"You dance like an angel," he said, holding her close and making her feel more cherished than she'd ever felt in her life.

With their masks on, they seemed like two other people. She wanted them to be those people forever, but she was quickly reminded that even here the prince had obligations.

He danced with beautiful young women and elegant older ones, while she was shuffled around the floor by an army of moist-palmed, buff and hardy men.

She wanted to be with Max, no one but Max. She watched him whenever she could and longed for him every moment of the evening. When he was able to claim her for a dance, she was in paradise.

At midnight everyone removed the glittery satin masks, and she asked Max to tuck hers in his pocket.

"For a souvenir," she said, saddened because it was him she wanted to keep, not a little party favor.

"Would you like mine, too?"

"Yes, please." Maybe she'd frame them so some part of them would always be together.

He escorted her to a sumptuous midnight buffet where he fed her caviar on a heart-shaped cracker and edged his chair so close their legs intertwined under cover of the linen tablecloth.

Afterward, the orchestra played again, and all the important demanding people who'd kept them apart earlier in the evening seemed to vanish. Or maybe they were restrained by the way the prince held his fiancée when they danced.

"It's been a wonderful night," he said, holding her against his shoulder as they danced.

"Yes, it has."

"I don't want it to end."

"I guess everything has to sooner or later."

She wanted him to deny it. The princess thing wasn't impossible. She was willing to dance with clods in hiking boots and eat octopus eyes on crackers if that was what it took. Albert could give her lessons on how to walk, talk, and arrange flowers for the palace tables. She was more than agreeable to having Schwanstein history drilled into her until her brain suffered information overload. Why couldn't Max see she had potential if nothing else?

"I'm afraid it's time to leave," he said all too soon. He held her tighter.

"If only they'd play one more piece."

He didn't ask why. With a flick of his finger, he brought Hans to his side.

"Please request one more waltz and give the orchestra my compliments," he said.

Max's arms closed around her, and she knew this was the happiest moment of her life.

## ❧ 8 ❧

After the ball, Cinderella went back to sweeping the hearth, Leigh recalled as she walked toward the workout room in the basement of the Dallas Ali Baba Hotel. Now her own magical evening was over, and compared to sucking in soot, a little exercise wasn't so bad.

Of course, Cinderella eventually got her prince, and that wasn't going to happen to Leigh Bailey, reporter. So, while she had some time to kill, she might as well keep trim. All those fancy clothes had to fit for a few more days.

Maybe she'd dreamed the whole ball. Maybe Max had never asked for an extra waltz so he could hold her in his arms for a little longer.

"No way," she said under her breath. It had been as real as the warmth of his hands when he put on her shoe. Just thinking about the sensual way his hands had caressed her foot made her ache with longing.

Since the ball, nothing. Hans had walked her to her room afterward; Albert had occupied the seat beside the prince on the plane trip to Dallas. Max hadn't mentioned the Silver and Gold Ball not even once. It might never have happened.

At least he hadn't brought up the hospital. What explanation could she give for spying on him and running out so fast she'd lost her shoe?

The morning after, before they left for Dallas, she'd been upset by a newspaper article criticizing him for arriving late at the ball. When she mentioned it, he'd shrugged it off.

"If we really were engaged, you'd have to develop thicker skin," he'd told her.

She took it as his way of reminding her she wasn't princess material. As if she didn't know it.

She pushed open the heavy door that muffled the grunts and wheezes of body-conscious hotel guests and showed her room card to an attendant with pecs and abs to die for. Unfortunately, he also had a big beefy face and a pouty too-small mouth. Men just weren't looking good to her lately.

Except for one.

Max was working on a weight machine, his torso bare above the waist. A moist sheen accentuated his golden tan and matted the silky dark hairs that disappeared under low-slung trunks. His cute little navel invited her to tease it with her pinkie, and she had an alarming urge to kneel beside him and cradle her cheek on one of his muscular thighs.

I hate you, Prince Maximilian Augustus Frederick, she thought, tempted to leave before he saw her. How could he look so great and be so charming and not share in the feelings consuming her? Didn't he see what it was doing to her, pretending to be his fiancée and trying to be indifferent to the chemistry between them at the same time?

She had no one but herself to blame, and that made her even more upset. She hurried over to a rowing machine because it was placed so she wouldn't have to look in his direction.

Max, however, had seen her come in, and he knew she was pretending not to see him. What was the little wench trying to pull now? She kept him so off balance he felt like a prisoner on a roller coaster. Leigh's soft lips, sexy hips, and incredibly delightful chatter were all he could think about. He was in big trouble.

He forced himself to finish the repetitions he'd

begun, then stood and rubbed down his chest and arms with a towel, draping it around his neck. His trunks were sticking damply to his buttocks; he was too sweaty to approach a lady, but he was drawn to Leigh like iron to a magnet.

Hans was taking a turn in the sauna, and Fred was making small talk with the hotel's trainer. There was no one to distract him from approaching her.

He saw the energetic way she tugged on the oars, her shoulders knotting under a sleeveless top as she put all she had into her effort. There were exciting reserves of strength in her slender limbs, and he couldn't hold back an image of her legs locked around him in passion.

He'd been prepared to seduce her after the ball, but the foil-wrapped packets were still tucked away in one of his cases, unopened but not forgotten. He'd been confident of success, sure that her consent would be wholehearted enough to keep his honor intact.

It wasn't his promise not to take advantage of her that kept him from making love to her. Nor was it fear of rejection or recriminations. Those were reasons he could understand. What he felt was much more complicated. He felt protective, but at the same time he admired the way she could take care of herself. When he was near her, he was in an almost constant state of arousal, but the sight, sound, even the scent of other women left him totally indifferent.

Yesterday, when he'd tried to put distance between them by remaining aloof, speaking to her as little as possible, he suffered an even more intense longing. Separation was no solution for his yearning.

"Good morning, Leigh," he said, walking into her line of vision.

"Good morning, Your Highness." She didn't stop her rhythmic pulling.

"So formal. Have I done something to deserve it?"

She didn't look up, allowing him to watch the jut of her breasts and the way a loose strand of honey-gold hair clung to her cheek. What pleasure it would be to carry her into the sauna and slowly peel off her bright-blue leotard. He wanted to see her fair skin flush from the dry heat and grow even pinker under his caresses.

He wanted her. It was that simple—and so complex he felt powerless.

"I've no idea what you've done. Don't you have a meeting?" she asked nonchalantly.

"In an hour or so I'll be conferring with some venture capitalists interested in Schwanstein's high-tech potential. For a woman who loves to ask questions, you're amazingly adroit at evading them. When did I stop being Max?"

She looked up, running her gaze down the length of his torso. He felt seared by the directness of her stare. He had absolutely no prudishness about his body, but she made him feel exposed.

He yanked on the towel around his neck and pulled it free, letting it hang in front of him as he patted his face and throat.

"Do you get tired of royal courtesies?" She stopped rowing and sat motionless, looking up at him.

"Another question, instead of an answer."

"It's what I do best."

"I doubt that. You have other qualities—"

He clamped his mouth shut, knowing how it must feel to venture through a bog where every step could plunge you into quicksand.

"I'm going to ride the bike." She was quick and nimble, on her feet before he could offer his hand.

"Have you tried the sauna here?" he asked.

It was an invitation, and she knew it. They wouldn't have any privacy there, but he wanted to see her wrapped in a towel in the cleansing heat.

"Maybe later."

Maybe alone, she meant.

"It's hard not to see you through other people's eyes," she said.

"What do you mean?" He frowned, wondering why the workings of her mind fascinated him.

"Your title. Sometimes you seem so regal...not quite real."

"I assure you I have all the faults and weaknesses of our species."

"Do you want to come back to my room with me now?" His mouth went dry; his face stiffened, as though he'd just removed a very tight mask. He wanted to lie, to say something witty to defuse the tension between them, but he saw her soft pink lips and wavered.

"Yes, I do."

"But you won't."

"No."

"That wasn't an invitation. I just wondered."

"I didn't believe it was," he lied.

"You have responsibilities. You take them seriously. You wouldn't let yourself be late for a meeting."

"No." This wasn't a conversation he wanted to be having with her. "What will you do today?"

"I'd like to see the grassy knoll."

"I beg your pardon?"

"Where Kennedy was shot. Things are never what they seem, but sometimes they are, and sorting them out is harder than a black puzzle."

"Now I need to ask what a black puzzle is."

"A jigsaw puzzle, say of a black cat lying on a black bedspread."

"So they have to be matched by shape?"

"Yes, but there's not much difference in puzzle shapes. Sometimes the solution isn't worth the work involved."

"There isn't much you can do with a jigsaw puzzle when it's finished," he said.

"You can glue them, use them as place mats or wall hangings."

"I bow to your creative instincts."

"Is that permissible? For a prince to bow?"

He shook his head, bewildered by the direction of their conversation. They were using words to build a wall between them. He was surprised by her perceptiveness and confused by the intensity of his feelings. She told him she knew he couldn't give first priority to his own desires, but how could he convince himself of that? Did she have any idea how badly he wanted to take her in his arms and kiss her until the world around them faded into oblivion?

"When our engagement is over, I'll answer your questions," he said. "Now I have to prepare for my meeting. Enjoy your excursion. I'll be interested to hear about it." She watched him stride away, her throat tight with regret for what could never be, but that didn't dull her admiration. What was so special about his walk?

He did it the usual way, one foot in front of the other. It wasn't fair. How could he be cute and sexy with his shorts clinging to his wonderfully rounded bottom and still walk with dignity? He was everything a man should be—and he might as well come from Mars for all the good it did her.

She'd never been so mortified. She'd invited a prince to go to bed with her, and he'd turned her down.

She dragged herself onto the stationary bicycle and pedaled until her calves burned. This was nothing like her crush on Brad in high school or her brief but heady infatuation with Barry in college. Her only real affair, with Tom, had been comfortable, convenient, and not very exciting. They'd shared rent, had pleasant-enough sex when they were both in town at the same time, and parted on a reasonably friendly basis when he went gaga over a schoolteacher in Massachusetts.

She'd never experienced anything like this crazy obsession with the prince. She thought about him all the time and lay wide-eyed at night, fantasizing about being his bride. For the first time in years, she wanted advice from her mother. That was scary.

She finally stopped pedaling and limped away

from the training room. Pride decreed she do a Dallas tour if only to remind Max—and herself—she had a life. When he left, she still had a career, friends, ambitions, interests...

"Oh, shoot," she muttered to herself. "A black cat on a black sheet?" It was as bad as her bumper sticker. He probably thought her brain was made of marshmallow.

The meeting went well, no thanks to him, Max knew. Without a team of sharp lawyers backing him up, he would have floundered. His concentration was nil, his bargaining skills dulled. Leigh was with him all day in spirit, and he caught himself rethinking their conversations, trying to understand her appeal. It was like measuring mist. There was nothing he could hold in his hands or weigh on a scale, yet she affected everything he did.

He couldn't wait until she was scheduled to meet him for dinner with a Texas oil baron, a multimillionaire and potential investor, and his wife. The prospect of consuming several pounds of half-cooked beef at one of the city's famous steakhouses was bearable only because Leigh would be with him.

He called her room three times in the hour before

they were supposed to leave, more dejected each time she failed to answer. At the appointed hour, he ordered his bodyguards to meet him in the lobby and walked alone down the corridor to her room, this time on the same floor as his. What would he do if she hadn't returned from her excursion? Should he search for her? Would it mean something had happened to her? Would she leave him without a word?

He'd done all he could to keep her by his side during his travels. He couldn't command her—and he wouldn't beg her—to finish the trip if she was determined not to stay with him. Nor would he deny her the interview. She'd earned it. He knew how irksome and tedious royal duties were, especially for a woman with her independent ways.

Taking a deep breath, he knocked softly on her door, bracing himself to discover she wasn't there.

When the door flew open, he smiled with relief.

"I thought perhaps you weren't coming with me this evening."

"Why would you think that?"

"You didn't answer your phone."

"Are you the pest who called three times in ten minutes?"

"You heard and didn't pick it up?"

"After a day of doing Dallas, I needed a long soak

in a hot bath. I knew by the time I climbed out of the tub and dripped my way to the phone, the caller would've hung up."

Much as he'd love seeing her rise from her bath, flushed from the heat and languidly lovely, she was a delight now to his eyes, dressed in a champagne dress with short bell sleeves and a skirt that ended midthigh. A lightning pattern of sequins underscored her breasts and made an artfully jagged descent to the hem.

"How was your day?" he asked, forcing himself not to stare.

"I learned a lot, but the most bizarre was hearing all the wild theories about who had Kennedy killed. The driver of the tour bus has a theory I've never heard. He thinks Elvis was really working for the CIA—not totally preposterous because he was in the Army—"

"Excuse me for interrupting, but we do have a limo waiting," Max said, wishing he could spend the rest of the evening alone with her.

"Will my rain poncho look silly with this dress? It was starting to rain when I came back to the hotel."

"You won't get wet. The driver will have an umbrella."

"Of course. I forget how people rush to wait on you."

"That smacks of criticism. In your democratic zeal, you Americans forget how many jobs—well-paying jobs—depend on my lifestyle."

"I don't want to offend you, but really? Can you imagine how boring it must be for Hans and Fred to follow you around like a pair of mastiffs?"

"Their jobs are considered prestigious in my country. They are well paid and enjoy travel, fine food, good hotels..."

"No family life, no time for girlfriends or wives..."

"My visits abroad are important to my country's economy," he said stiffly, resenting the truth in what she said almost as much as her cheekiness in bringing it up.

"Uh-oh, you're angry with me," she said with a trace of contriteness.

"You have a right to express your opinions, however misguided they are."

"If you'd rather I don't go tonight..."

He put his hand on her upper arm and tried to ignore the softness of her skin and the firmness of the muscle under it.

"The reservations have been made."

"Yes, it's on the itinerary." She was angrier than he was, her words crackling in the quiet room.

"Tell me more about what you did today," he said, regretting the bad start to their evening.

"Unfortunately, I won't have any time for sightseeing here."

He guided her into the hallway with a light touch on her shoulder, pulling the door shut behind them.

"All right," she said, slightly mollified. "I heard another theory. The same space aliens who took Elvis kidnapped JFK."

"What else did you do?" He steered her toward the elevators, his hand resting lightly on the side of her waist.

"You're not really interested."

He'd never seen her pout like this, her lips pursing, the lower one protruding slightly more than the top. If ever a mouth invited a kiss...

"Do you ever consider the possibility that something isn't exactly what it seems?" she went on.

"I prefer to deal in facts. You can save the wild rumors for your magazine," he said, unused to women who challenged him and not sure how to deal with her.

"It's not that kind of magazine!"

She pushed his hand away and stopped walking, confronting him with hands on her hips, legs spread, eyes sparkling with anger. Her anger made his dissolve. Fighting wasn't at the top of the list of things he wanted to do with her.

"It was unthinking of me to make a remark about a magazine I've never read. I apologize."

"Just like that? You apologize?"

"Can we get on an elevator? The limo is waiting."

"I don't want your apology. I want to be mad at you."

"So you'll have an excuse not to go this evening?"

"No—I don't know. You make me absolutely crazy. I can't sort out where the prince ends and the man begins. You can be so judgmental..."

"Judgmental? Because I don't believe Elvis and JFK were abducted by extraterrestrials?"

To his relief—and delight—she laughed, genuine heartfelt laughter that compelled him to join in. Surprising himself and her, he took her in his arms and kissed her, long and hard and a little desperately. There wasn't time for this to go anywhere, and he was probably ruining her lipstick and smearing it all over his mouth, but heaven help him, he needed her. He wanted her.

"Excuse me, please," a stranger's voice interrupted.

They were blocking the corridor, forcing a silver-haired couple to get their attention in order to pass.

"Very sorry," Max murmured, stepping aside and taking Leigh with him.

"I liked that apology," she teased softly. "It was

worth the fight. I should make you angry more often."

She gave him a sly little smile and reached up to touch his mouth with her fingertips.

"You're wearing most of my lipstick. Should we go back to the room and clean up?" she asked.

"Regretfully, I must get to this dinner." He pulled out his handkerchief and rubbed his lips.

"I wasn't suggesting otherwise," she said sweetly —too sweetly.

"I like you without lipstick. Your lips are naturally rosy." He folded the square of linen and wiped her mouth, as well.

"Say it," she challenged.

He looked perplexed. "Say what?"

"Admit that was the best kiss you've ever had, maybe the best kiss ever. Tell me something. Can't you fend off potential princesses by now? I'm tired of this...this game."

"Do you want to go home, forget your article?"

"No way, Your Highness! You promised."

"I did, didn't I? And so did you." He placed his hands on the striped wallpaper behind her, trapping her between his arms. "And you're playing a cat-and-mouse game yourself, making up the rules as you go. What do you really want to know about me, Leigh?"

He didn't let her answer; he didn't want to hear

about her dedication as a writer or her career aspirations. He kissed her one more time, hoping she'd suffer in some small way for the denial that was driving him crazy.

"We have to go," he said.

"Yes."

She broke free and walked toward the elevator, her high heels throwing her off-kilter just enough to make her backside sway provocatively.

He took a deep breath and followed. It was going to be a long evening.

## 9

L eigh watched the rain strike the window of her hotel room and made bets with herself whenever two drops raced side by side to the bottom. She picked the wrong drop three consecutive times and gave up. Talk about backing losers.

She felt like a loser herself this morning. She knew enough about Max to write a book, partly thanks to his great-aunt Lucinda, but he was still a mystery in all the important ways. Why did his eyes generate enough heat to melt ice cream when he looked at her? Why did he run hot and cold, charming one minute and aloof the next?

And most puzzling of all, if he needed a wife and an heir to ensure his country's future, why was he using her to keep women at bay?

She didn't know much about royal mating habits,

but Max seemed too responsible to stay single forever. Maybe his marriage was already arranged; after all, his family must have expected his cousin Darcy to fill the role of temporary fiancée. Or maybe this was his last fling before he settled down with an appropriate wife.

The endless round of business meetings and social engagements didn't seem like much of a fling, but she had no way of knowing whether his evening ended when hers did.

Why had he dragged her into this?

"Dragged!" she said aloud, suffering from a painful flash of objectivity. "I leaped at the chance to be with him."

She turned from the window, sick of dreary weather and gloomy thoughts. She hadn't felt the sun on her face since her trip to the grassy knoll two days ago. The "Case of the Missing Evening Gowns" in Chicago seemed like fun compared to the demands Dallas was making on Max. She'd never been here before, but she had a feeling she was missing the best the city had to offer.

Their itinerary for that evening listed a street festival in a nearby town. She was thumbing through a visitors' magazine, looking for ways to kill time until then when Albert came to her room.

"I must apologize, Miss Bailey. I misunderstood

what was required for the informal affair this evening. His Highness wishes to go in Western wear."

"That's no problem. I have some jeans with me."

The valet looked slightly shocked. "I beg your pardon, miss, but trousers wouldn't be appropriate. I've arranged for you to visit the Western apparel shop in the hotel. You can select boots and a hat there, as well as the rest of your costume. If you like, I'll accompany you."

"I wouldn't want to keep you from your other responsibilities," she said.

"Very kind of you, miss." He looked relieved. "Please charge your purchases to your room. The prince will expect you to secure the nicest possible cattle-woman garb."

"Dress like a cowgirl, you mean. I won't let you down, Albert. I'll go whole hog."

"Whole hog." He obviously found the phrase distasteful but was man enough to bear it. He backed out of her room and closed the door behind him.

A few minutes later she was on an elevator, intent on following Albert's orders. She loved hotel lobbies. They were the best places for people watching, except perhaps zoos, where the animals usually had more dignity than the spectators. Hotel shops, though, had always been strictly for browsing.

She felt extravagant if she bought so much as a

package of breath mints in one, but Albert still intimidated her enough to make her follow his instructions to the letter. If Max wanted a good ole gal, he'd get one.

The clerk in the Western-wear store had dark sultry eyes and coal-black hair pulled into a bun, but her accent was West Texas, peppered with casual endearments.

"You're the prince's fiancée," she said enthusiastically. "His valet said to expect you."

Leigh's plan to kill a couple of hours looking around and trying on clothes was scuttled. She had to endure the royal treatment, which meant the clerk hovered, made suggestions, and brought armloads of skirts, blouses, and dresses into the dressing room, regardless of Leigh's state of undress.

The woman oozed politeness, but Leigh felt as though she were under a magnifying glass being checked for cellulite, split ends, and any flaws that would make good coffee-break gossip.

Maybe she'd do the same thing if their places were reversed. Maybe Max's jaundiced view of her profession was somewhat justified. People liked to read about the shortcomings of famous people. They probably felt more satisfied with their own lives when they learned that even the rich and beautiful suffered their share of unhappiness. But was it a public service or a violation of privacy to dig out hidden faults?

Now that she thought about it, Max seemed to take the public clamor in stride. He resented her professional interest in him more than the inaccurate and downright false reports in the newspapers.

"Pretty, but not what I have in mind," Leigh finally said, handing back the whole pile of grossly overpriced garments. "Maybe I'll just think about it for a while."

"We have some beautiful silver belts—"

"Thank you, but I don't have time to decide on anything now." She hurried out of the store feeling mean-spirited in the face of the clerk's obvious disappointment.

After getting her rain poncho from her room, she grabbed the first cab she could while the doorman was busy with a couple of Japanese businessmen.

"Take me to a Western-wear shop," she told the driver. "One where working people shop, not a fancy tourist trap."

She watched the meter tick with some alarm, but the cabbie did what she wanted. He stopped at a huge building with the ambiance of a warehouse and bargains advertised on the windows in neon paint. She asked him to come back in an hour.

"Better make it two, lady. Takes some looking to find what you want in there."

She agreed and was glad of it when she hurried out two hours later with purchases that strained her credit card but buoyed up her self-esteem. She could still dress herself, thank you very much, Your Highness.

The rain stopped for a while in the late afternoon but began again while Leigh dressed for the evening in her new duds. She'd settled for a little dress with a ruffle that left lots of leg showing between the hem and her rhinestone boots. She hoped the clear sparkly stones wouldn't fall out, but she loved them because they complemented the dangly earrings she'd worn to the ball.

She teased her straight strands until she had big hair and topped the dress with a white vest stamped with cattle brands. She'd never worn a cowboy hat before, but she punched the white felt a few times to give it a used look. She'd passed up the rhinestone sunglasses and now regretted it.

She couldn't wait to see Max's reaction to her getup.

"Buster, you've bitten off more than you can handle this time," she said in her best John Wayne imitation.

She was standing in a cloud of hairspray when he

knocked. With a last pat on her stiff hair, she put on the hat and ambled to the door in the surprisingly comfortable boots.

"Howdy, stranger," she said, owing more to Mae West than John Wayne.

He really looked like a stranger—and a heart-stopping one at that. His plaid flannel shirt and fringed suede jacket were classics of the Old West, but his jeans were stone-washed and designer-sleek, hugging his thighs and leaving no gender doubts. The cuffs were outside his tooled leather boots and, ever the gentleman, he had hat in hand.

"What a waste," he said with a whistle.

"I beg your pardon! I bought these clothes myself, so you don't have to worry about waste. I happen to like them."

"I happen to love them." He stepped inside and closed the door. "Unfortunately, the street festival has been canceled. That's what I meant by waste—I would love showing off my cowgirl-fiancée."

"I thought maybe it would be moved inside." She was surprised by the intensity of her disappointment. After all, it was only another social event, not an enchanted ball.

"No, we're free for the evening."

"Don't feel you have to entertain me."

"I'm entertained just by seeing you. You're a

chameleon—no matter what you wear, it's perfect for you."

"Thank you." She wasn't used to his compliments. She hoped her made-up cheeks disguised her blush.

"We still have to eat," he said, taking the glow off his compliment by suggesting he was there only because he was hungry. "What would you say to trying the hotel cuisine? It's not a night to go looking for a restaurant. I thought we could order room service."

"No."

"Very well, there are several restaurants in the hotel that look promising. If you'd like to select one..."

"No, thank you."

He kept his cool; she had to concede that. Or else he didn't really care whether she joined him for dinner.

"You're leaving me no choice but to dine alone. I took your comments about my bodyguards to heart. I've given both of them—Albert, too—a free evening."

"You give up too easily." She pretended to pout. "I didn't dress up like a rodeo queen to hang around the Ali Baba Hotel."

He smiled broadly, the high-magnitude glow on

his face throwing off heat she could feel all the way to her rhinestone boots.

"You wouldn't say no to some local color?" he asked. "Not if it means real barbecue sauce, the kind that burns your tongue and drips down your chin."

"Ribs we yank apart with our hands?"

"Chicken we eat with our fingers."

"Have you ever tried dancing in a row?" he asked.

"Line dancing! No, but I've never had boots before, either." She grinned.

"Do you know a place?"

"Nope, but I know how to find one."

"The concierge?"

"A cabdriver. That's how I found a place to buy these." She twirled with outstretched arms to give him the full effect of her outfit.

"I'm convinced."

"I'm wearing my poncho. Do you want to get a raincoat?"

"With a hat like this, ma'am," he said, plunking on his, "a man is his own umbrella."

"Can we do this? Won't you be recognized? It won't be much fun if we can't escape notice."

"Leave it to me." He ducked into the bathroom and ran water while she wondered what he was doing.

When he came out, his hair was slicked back and

most of his shirt was unbuttoned. She longed to run her hands over the broad expanse of his chest.

"This may not fool everyone, but it will confuse enough people to let us make our getaway."

He was good at sneaking out, she noted. They got off the elevator on the second floor, walked down, hurried out an exit in a wing of the hotel used for conferences, and caught a taxi just entering the long drive to the main entrance.

"James Bond couldn't make a cleaner escape," she teased. "Were you trained in evasion techniques, or is it a natural gift?"

"Trial and error." He took off his damp hat and put it on the seat of the cab, making it necessary to sit closer to her.

"We want to line dance and eat barbecue," Leigh told the driver who'd just made a probably illegal U-turn and was ready to reenter traffic. "But not a touristy place."

The driver was young with greasy blond hair curling over the collar of his denim jacket. He worked a wad of bubble gum thoughtfully over the tip of his tongue.

"No place like that around here," he said. "There's about seventeen hotels in this square mile." He waved his arm and changed lanes, followed by an irate honk from a semi.

"We're good for a half hour of cab time. Is there a place in that range?"

"It doesn't matter—" Max began, leaning forward like a man about to take charge.

She tugged on his sleeve and shook her head just enough to give him a warning.

"There's Logan's Saloon, but they get a rough crowd. Noisy place. Sometimes there's some fighting."

"Tourists?" Leigh asked.

"Naw, not in that neighborhood."

"Where else—" Max began again, but she interrupted.

"Take us there." She looked at Max to see if he really objected, but he grinned and shrugged, letting her know he was ready to follow her, at least this once.

"You got it." The cabbie swerved across two lanes, jamming Leigh against the door and throwing Max practically on her lap.

"Sorry. Are you all right?" Max put space between them, but not much.

"Guess seat belts are called for."

She reached down but could only find one strap.

"Here, let me." He slid forward and dug a buckle out of the crevice between the seat and the back, then reached across her lap to take the one she was holding. He couldn't make the ends meet.

"Either I've gained weight or those don't go together," she said, wondering if he could feel her breasts through the suede arm of his jacket.

"Sorry."

He dipped into the crevice again, this time coming up with a tangle of belts and a candy bar wrapper.

"You've hit garbage. Forget it."

"No, I believe in taking precautions."

Was he talking about seat belts...or something else? The question made her nerves tingle.

He reached on either side of her, somehow managing to sort out the tangle behind her back, and brought two matching ends together dead center over her tummy. In the process he tickled her tailbone, checked out the circumference of her waist, and raised her skirt six inches. This was a side of the prince she hadn't experienced.

"I'm well protected now, thank you," she said, removing his hand from her thigh.

Ordinarily she'd have no objection whatsoever to the location of his hand. In fact, she felt as malleable as kid's clay.

She was quivering, and her mind was doing flip-flops, imagining those fingers on her skin, doing wonderful things in all the right places. But she wasn't his to fondle. No way, Maximilian Augustus Frederick. It would be hard enough when this charade ended. She didn't want her memory of the ball sullied by some meaningless groping in the back seat of a cab.

Meaningless for him, that is. That was the problem.

"Aren't you going to wear a seat belt?" she asked him.

"No, it's not necessary." He was angry with himself, not her, and immediately regretted his harsh tone.

"You're the one with the fate of a nation dependent on this cabbie's driving skills," she said in a haughty whisper.

He'd tried to fondle her like a schoolboy, and now she was scolding him like a nanny. The only way this relationship could sink lower was for him to reveal how he really felt about her—and have her use it in an article.

Words failed him. He grabbed two straps and clicked them together in his lap with a snort of disgust at himself.

"You did it again—harrumph."

"I did?" He was wrong about sinking lower—now he felt ridiculous. Maybe, in spite of his attempts to be a caring considerate person, he was really only a royal bore.

He hadn't been tormented by self-doubt like this since he'd started shaving. Was this the man Leigh saw, the one she wanted to expose in her magazine? Or was he exaggerating everything because he was overwhelmed by his feelings and plagued by doubts about hers? She was his Lorelei, a sultry siren he couldn't resist even if it meant shipwreck and disaster as it had in the old legend.

Not only that, he was being melodramatic, a weakness inherited from his royal grandfather, God rest his soul. Usually Max suppressed this tendency, but here he was, in search of a fantasy of freedom— dressed as an American cowboy, master of his domain and free to love a woman of his own choosing. He almost told the driver to turn around, but if he changed his mind about the escapade, he'd lose this precious opportunity to be alone with Leigh.

"We'll play a game," she said. "If you harrumph one more time tonight, you have to pay a penalty."

"What penalty?"

"That's for me to decide."

"Only if I transgress..."

"Of course."

"Since my— What do you call it?"

"Harrumph."

"Since my harrumph offends you, I'll play your game. Will I be allowed to name my reward if I win?"

"I guess that's only fair," she said reluctantly.

"Until midnight then. Do you agree?"

"Until midnight." She made it sound like a solemn pact. The cab deposited them in front of a sprawling log building with a gaudy neon sign on the roof: Logan's Saloon. What he could see of the parking lot offered him a view of acres of pickup trucks.

When he opened the door, a blast of sound hit them like exhaust from a jet. He'd expected a country band; he wasn't prepared for music amplified enough to make the walls vibrate. He nearly backed out, but he looked down at Leigh, her cheeks flushed with excitement and her lips turned upward in an enchanting smile. He'd follow this woman into a bear cave.

"How many?"

The hostess wore pink boots, a ruffled black skirt up to her panty line, and a stretchy halter top that didn't flatter her huge breasts. She looked all of eighteen. He wanted to send her home to wash off the overdone makeup and put on decent clothes. He'd thought he was still young at thirty-two, but maybe he was turning into his father. But not tonight.

"Just two," he replied.

The girl led them to a high table with a round shiny black top and two stools placed across from each other.

"I guess we perch here," Leigh said, stepping on a chair rung to wriggle onto the seat.

He climbed up, too, and leaned forward, elbows on the table. The light was dim, but her eyes were like pools in a dense forest, deep and mysterious with sparkling green glints. He was drowning in those depths. He reached out, took her hand, and brought it slowly to his lips.

This was the prince who'd held her in his arms at the ball. He gently touched her fingers with his mouth, parting them, caressing with his lips.

"I'm glad you came out with me," he said—or at least that was what she thought he said. The music was ear-shattering. If they were going to communicate, they'd need sign language or a pad of paper.

He solved the problem by moving his stool next to hers, sitting so close he could speak directly into her ear. His words tickled—or so she told herself, not ready to admit that the wonderful tingling sensation radiating down her throat and making her breasts throb was part of his magic.

He ordered wine without consulting her and got a carafe of bitter red stuff that puckered her mouth.

"Terrible," he said, rolling a sip over his tongue like a man testing a good vintage.

"Vile."

"I'll send it back."

"No." She held out the juice glass that came with it and clinked it against his. "We'll get used to the taste."

He gave her a choice on the menu. They ordered the house special for two: chicken and ribs with all the fries they could eat. It came with sauce so tangy the wine started to taste mellow. The waitress tied paper bibs on them, and they were grease-spattered and spotted with bright-red sauce by the time they finished.

Then they danced. Max was born with wings on his feet. He stood watching on the sidelines for all of two minutes, then pulled her out to join the bobbing, ducking, prancing, hooting crowd. She tried to follow and got out of step and out of line, but he took her fingers in his, holding them up, and his natural grace seemed to flow through her.

They didn't stop until the band took a break and the place was oddly silent—for all of thirty seconds.

Then recorded music started wailing through overhead speakers, and the slow dancers stampeded the floor.

There were old folks and young in all sizes, shapes, and degrees of skill. Over Max's shoulders she saw lip-to-lip dancing, necking set to music, and a skinny cowboy who seemed to be dancing with two women, switching back and forth between them in rhythm to a plaintive song about infidelity. A portly couple danced with the grace of ballerinas, and a wizened old lady with pure-white hair was leading a gawky young man around the floor with audible instructions.

It wasn't the Silver and Gold Ball, but Leigh was enjoying herself more than she could have imagined.

"I love this," she said.

"I love you," he said.

At least that was what she thought he said. She couldn't ask him to repeat it. Maybe she'd only imagined it. Maybe the words came from the sound system. That was probably it. She must have heard the words from the male vocalist, whose accent was as foreign to her as Max's.

He was holding her so close their knees were bumping and their thighs rubbing. What he was thinking about her probably had nothing to do with love and a whole lot to do with lust.

She was dancing with a prince, and she envied every woman who swirled past who could go home with a man she loved.

But she'd have to say goodbye forever to Max, and she didn't know if she could live without this wonderful, beautiful man who was holding her so close she could feel the pounding of his heart, hear the echo of her own pulse.

She was breathless, her thoughts jumbled. And then he kissed her.

No big deal. People were kissing all over the place, stealing little pecks, doing calisthenics with their lips, exchanging romantic caresses with their mouths. It was probably catching: monkey see, monkey do.

Max did. They stopped in the middle of a crowd of enthusiastic dancers, making people flow around them like stream water diverted by a big boulder, and he really kissed her. He made her lips pulsate and sent shock waves to her groin.

He filled her mouth with his tongue and did indescribable things that made her melt. She clung to him and tried to kiss him back, but he overpowered her; this was his kiss. The longer it went on, the longer she wanted it to last.

Something changed. She opened her eyes to find them virtually alone on the dance floor.

"Max." She pushed him, gently and reluctantly, and heard the snickers and the outright laughter.

The music had stopped, and they hadn't.

"Way to go, fella!"

"Hey, I'll take one, too, cowboy!"

Leigh wanted to sink through the floor. Max put his arm around her shoulders and kissed her once more, this time for the crowd. He got applause; she got whistles. Or maybe it was the other way around. They walked off the floor and doubled over in laughter. Finally, he hoisted her onto the stool by their table and gave her a congratulatory hug.

"You handled that like a queen," he said. "Will you forgive me?"

"I'll give it some thought." But all she could think was: Is he as shell-shocked as I am?

He ordered white wine that had the bouquet of cider vinegar, and they toasted everything from the Dallas Cowboys to the inventor of the high-heeled boot.

"To the most beautiful woman in the world," he said, raising his squat little glass and not waiting for her to click hers against it.

Were they tipsy? The cabdriver must have thought so when, much later, he drove them back to the hotel. But he was all smiles when Max handed him a fifty-dollar bill and told him to keep the change.

"You're too extravagant!" she chided as they hurried into the hotel. "A couple of dollars would have been plenty."

"You're too frugal. I told you to charge a few clothes to your room, and you bought your own."

"I can buy my own clothes."

"You certainly can. I love what you're wearing."

There was that word again: love. She didn't want to hear that he loved her cowgirl skirt or her rhinestone boots, but there was no way to ask if he'd really said, "I love you," earlier in the evening.

"Did Albert buy those jeans for you?" she asked.

"Absolutely not!"

He laughed so hard she started laughing with him. She saw the concierge frown as they passed his desk, and a dignified couple made a disparaging remark about drunkenness.

"You're going to get us kicked out of the hotel," she warned, still giggling.

"I'm not intoxicated. Wine has never made me feel this way. It's being with you."

"I'm glad." She lowered her voice to a whisper because he was practically shouting. "Let's catch the elevator."

"Let's do that!"

He literally swept her off her feet and over his shoulder, her head hanging behind him. She squealed in protest.

"Max! Stop! You can't... Put me down."

He did as the elevator door slid shut.

Without noticing whether anyone else was in the car, he gathered her in his arms and began where they'd left off on the dance floor.

Leigh reached behind him and pushed the button for their floor.

They were alone in the elevator...

## 10

"The evening doesn't have to end." It wasn't the wine talking. Max had never wanted anything more than to keep her with him tonight. What would it be like to make love to her as the elevator rose from floor to floor? What would it be like to make love to her all night long?

"Everything ends sometime."

She sounded sad enough to raise his hopes. He knew she had fire and passion behind her cool beautiful exterior, but he didn't know how to ignite it.

Her hair framed her face like the halo on a Renaissance Madonna when she took off her hat, and he was awestruck by the luminous quality of her beauty. Then the bell chimed, and the elevator opened.

They reached her door too quickly, and he groped for words to keep her from leaving him.

"Some coffee perhaps?" he asked hopefully.

"I tried making some in my room. It tasted like burned rubber."

"Coffee isn't really what I want."

"I didn't think it was." Her words were playful, but she avoided meeting his eyes.

"I have my room card here." She reached into a deep pocket of her rain poncho. "No, I must have put it in the other one."

She checked both pockets twice, as though a thorough search would make the missing keycard reappear.

"My money is gone, too. I had a ten-dollar bill, a tissue, and the card. I've been robbed!"

"You left your poncho hanging on the back of the chair while we danced. It's my fault. I should have warned you against pickpockets. It only takes them an unguarded instant to relieve you of your property."

"I know without being warned. Where was my head? I'm usually careful. At least I took the card out of the hotel folder. There's no way the thief can know the room number or even the hotel. But my spare is locked inside my room."

She sounded truly distressed, but he knew her

well enough to realize she could handle a major crisis. This was only a minor inconvenience.

"Don't be angry with yourself," he said soothingly. "It's a small loss."

"It's embarrassing. I expect better of myself."

"Don't be embarrassed." He put his arm around her shoulders. "I'll call the desk from my room and have a replacement sent up. I'll take the blame, say I was carrying your card for you."

"No, I should go down and explain it myself."

He bent to kiss her cheek, intending to reassure her with a platonic gesture, but she turned her head at that instant. His lips grazed hers, and he felt a surge of desire so powerful he enveloped her in his arms without conscious thought.

She seemed to melt, and he kissed her as he'd never kissed anyone.

"Come to my room," he said, looking down at her face.

She covered her mouth with the back of her hand and stared at him with stunned eyes, as though she'd lost the ability to comprehend.

"I'll call the desk from there," he said, willing to promise anything to keep her with him.

"That would be nice of you," she said in a halting voice, not sounding at all convinced.

He guided her down the corridor to his door and

reached into his hip pocket. Much to his relief, his wallet was still there. His fingers felt thick and clumsy, and he inserted the card upside down on the first try, getting the red light that denied access.

"Your card doesn't work."

"It does if I use it properly."

He forced himself to focus on the random holes in the plastic, this time doing it right. The green light flickered, and he opened the door, snapped on a light, and stepped aside to let her enter.

"This is practically like my room," she said.

"You sound surprised. What were you expecting?"

"A suite, I guess. With Albert standing in the vestibule to take our coats and your bodyguards at attention on either side of the..." She hesitated.

"Bed?" He turned away so she wouldn't see him smile at her discomfort.

"You have a king-size."

"Don't you?"

"No, but I don't need one. I'm a very quiet sleeper. I stay on one pillow even if there are two others beside it."

Her cheeks were bright pink, and he marveled that a woman as worldly as Leigh could still blush in a man's bedroom. She intrigued him in more ways than he could count.

"I remember. You gave your men the night off," she said.

"They have their own rooms."

"Of course."

She shrugged, but he wasn't fooled. She was too curious about the lifestyle of a prince not to have questions about his personal habits.

"I shave myself, wash my own back, and dress myself. Does that answer some of your questions?"

"I didn't ask!"

He ignored her protest, too amused to give up the game. "Albert does take care of laundering, cleaning, and laying out my clothes. He keeps my shoes shined —I'm a fanatic about that—and makes sure the room is done to his satisfaction. He keeps my appointment schedule, checks messages, and shops for me. I sometimes give him the odd job, too."

"How convenient for you," she said dryly, fixing her eyes on a nondescript floral print hanging over the bed.

"He also tactfully rebukes me when I'm impatient and scolds me when I deserve it. He's frightfully good at holding up a mirror to my faults. He was, by the way, originally appointed to his post by my father, but I've grown too fond of him to consider employing anyone else."

"Why are we talking about Albert? I need to get

into my room."

"I'm talking about him—you aren't. And it's only a shameless ploy to keep you here as long as possible. If it's not working, I can try something else."

She was rooted to a spot halfway between the door and the bed.

"Max..."

She turned toward him, her eyes meeting his in a silent exchange that told him all he needed to know.

Leigh watched him walk toward her, seeing him in slow motion as she tried to think of a reason to rush out of the room. Then he took her in his arms, and her mind went blank.

"May I kiss you?" he asked softly.

She hadn't expected him to ask. Her lips were parted, and she lifted her face to his, surprised to realize he was waiting for her consent.

"A good-night kiss would be very nice," she murmured.

"I don't think I can." He made no move to kiss her but didn't release her.

"Oh?"

"If I kiss you now, you'll spend the night in my arms."

"Don't count on it." It was a feeble protest.

"It's destiny."

"Oh, Max!" She couldn't help laughing. "That

sounds like dialogue from a 1950s movie—a cast of thousands and Victor Mature fighting single-handedly against an army. I love those oldies, but I don't want to live one."

He released her and stalked to the window, staring out the rain-streaked glass to the blur of lights below.

"Is that how you see me, a throwback of a prince with a comical little kingdom?"

"Oh, no! Nothing like that. You're special—you're wonderful. I've never met a man like you."

"Come here." It was a command, and not a gentle, coaxing one.

"I apologize for laughing, but that doesn't mean you can give me orders."

"Come here." He didn't soften his tone a bit, and now she was annoyed.

"I'm going down to the desk to get a new card." It was only a threat; she was rooted to the spot, too intrigued by the man to walk away.

"Leigh, I wish you wouldn't do that quite yet."

"Oh, Max."

Her lower lip was trembling. Why couldn't he be a plumber or a professor or a pig farmer? Anyone but a prince. Even when he was arrogant, he touched her in places she'd never known existed. This was her chance to walk, to put him out of her life.

She took one unsteady step backward, her eyes

still riveted on his face. She was making the right decision. The closer they became, the worse it would be when he left her. If they made love, her heart would turn to ice and shatter in a million pieces when he turned his back on her to marry a suitable princess.

"Come here, please." His voice was so low she could just make out his words, but there was no mistaking the passion or the longing. He was begging her to stay as surely as if he'd dropped to his knees.

"It's not a good idea." Her chest ached; she nearly stammered the words.

"Yes, it is."

"We'll both regret it."

"No, never." There wasn't an iota of doubt in his voice.

"I wish I'd never met you."

"You don't mean that."

She didn't. It was frightening to realize he meant more to her than anything in the world.

"It has to be your choice," he said. "I gave my word not to betray your trust. Come to me, Leigh, darling. Free me from my promise."

"You're free."

"Not until you come willingly into my arms."

"Stop it!" She didn't know what she wanted him to stop. Tempting her? Wanting her?

She was still wearing her poncho with the empty pockets. The thief had even taken her tissue, so she didn't dare cry. She was hot and bothered, and the boots pinched after all that dancing. She shrugged out of the poncho and let it fall to the floor, but her face still felt feverishly warm.

"We should talk about this," she cautiously suggested.

"Words are the tools of your trade, aren't they?" he asked in a suspicious voice.

"Yes, but they'll also help me understand how you feel—and how I feel."

"How I feel?" He sounded bemused. "I can't compare the way I feel about you to anything else in my experience. I'm light-headed..."

"That's only the wine."

"I can't turn a corner, enter a room, look down a crowded street without hoping I'll see you."

"I sit in hotel lobbies hoping you'll walk past," she said.

"I wake up in the morning trying to think of excuses to cancel all my engagements so I can be with you."

"I live for the moment when you come to my door."

She knew the space between them was shrinking even though neither had moved.

"I ache to hold you in my arms," he said.

"I'm dying to be there." She took a tentative step toward him.

"Nothing in life is simple."

Was he warning her? She didn't care. His eyes were dark beacons showing her the way she wanted to go.

"I'm not afraid." She tried to convince herself.

"Leigh, come to me." It was still an order, but she heard sweet longing and desperate need in his quiet words.

"I'm going to regret this." She took two more tentative steps.

"Not tonight you aren't."

She moistened her lips with the tip of her tongue, too focused on the open V of his shirt and the snug fit of his jeans to say more. Everything about him suggested strength: his straight regal nose, his unwavering gaze, his powerful chin line, the swell of muscles under his jacket. Her mouth was dry and her heart racing, but she let herself believe him. She was going to dream about this moment for the rest of her life.

"Darling," she whispered.

She was in his arms at the foot of the bed. He hadn't waited by the window. His kiss was sweeter because he'd met her halfway.

His lips brushed against her closed lids, then moved across her brow. Panic penetrated her euphoria. She wasn't ready for this. She was wearing way too much makeup, and her heavily sprayed hair was matted. If they made love—when they made love—he'd see her at her worst.

His mouth was on target again, giving her slow sensual kisses, but she couldn't surrender to the pleasure. She looked horrible, and the smoky atmosphere of Logan's Saloon still clung to her clothes. She was Cinderella in her hearth-cleaning rags, not a desirable partner for a prince. "I should go to my room, take a shower."

"You can't get in," he murmured in her ear, doing something wonderful with his tongue.

"I'll call the desk."

"Don't even think of it."

He slipped off her cowgirl vest and spread his hands across her back, kneading away her tension.

"Just long enough to shower. I'll come back. I promise." His fingers were busy with the row of little metal buttons on the front of her dress. They parted like magic for him, and he gently cupped her lace-clad breasts.

"Beautiful," he said so softly she had to strain to hear. If she didn't assert herself now, he was going to stroke her sticky hair. She wanted to be perfect for him. This was only going to happen once, and she didn't want it ruined by makeup smeared on the pillowcase.

"Max, you have to let me go back to my room."

"If you're concerned about protection"—he released her and crossed to the large mirrored dresser —"I'm guilty of hoping something would happen between us."

He held up a bunch of foil-wrapped packets, then put them on the bedside table, giving her just enough time to retreat to his bathroom.

"I'm going to take a shower. I need to wash away Logan's Saloon," she said firmly, then shut the door and clicked the lock.

Was she crazy? She didn't do one-night stands. In fact, she didn't do much at all. Max was out of her league. She didn't want to be his playmate, and genuine royal princes didn't marry women they picked up on the highway in a storm.

She needed to clear her head and think about what was happening. She didn't want bad wine to make the call for her.

Tugging off the boots with a sigh of relief, she wiggled her toes and tried not to think about Max's dreamy eyes and sheltering arms. She was in a tight spot, torn between letting her heart or her head rule. Compromise was out of the question this time.

A few minutes later she stepped into the bathtub and let water from the shower nozzle stream over her head. She soaped her hair vigorously with the hotel's shampoo and closed her eyes to let the jet of water rinse away the suds.

Her heart stopped for an instant when she heard a noise, then she remembered locking the door. Anyway, this wasn't the Bates Motel. A man wasn't going to burst through the shower curtain and—

"*Eeeeek!*"

"Darling, I'm sorry for frightening you." Max stepped into the tub and caught her in his arms. "I thought you heard me."

"I locked the door."

"Hotel bathrooms have flimsy locks in case a guest slips in the bath."

"You picked the lock."

She wanted to be furious with him, but oh, he was gorgeous. His shoulders were sleek and muscular, his chest breathtaking, his waist slim, his tummy flat...

She embarrassed herself by looking lower and gasped.

He stepped closer and let water cascade over him.

She'd never taken a shower with a man. Did she wash him? Did he wash her? What if...? Did they...? Would he...?

He reached around her and took a large bar of

pale-yellow soap from a niche in the tile wall.

"My own special blend," he said, rubbing it between his hands until he had a fistful of suds.

He wasn't... He was.

His slippery hands caressed her back and shoulders and slid down her arms, covering her with wonderfully scented bubbles. Then he reached around her and slowly soaped her front.

Nothing compared to the ecstasy of his fingers on her breasts, teasing her nipples into hard, aching peaks. Gradually he made her forget her inhibitions until, when he went down on one knee, she trusted him implicitly.

"Oh, oh, oh. Oh, yes."

She didn't know she was speaking out loud. She buried her fingers in the wet strands of his hair and was lost in sensation until he rose, gave her a playful tap on her bottom, and placed the big oval of soap in her hand.

She couldn't... She didn't know how. But she did.

Everywhere.

Water slides in amusement parks would always seem tame after this. She reveled in the firmness of his body. She found his soft spots and was surprised and excited by the contrast.

When he reached behind her again and turned off the water, she was disappointed.

"It's only begun," he promised, looking down at her with solemn eyes.

He stepped out first, then offered his hand and wrapped her in the folds of the big white towel he held for her.

He dried her with slow gentle pats, then squeezed water from her hair and used his own comb to work out the tangles. When she reached for a fresh towel to reciprocate, he smiled sheepishly and scooped her off her feet.

"The air dried me, and this endurance test has to end soon. You've had me in knots for longer than any man should have to suffer."

"You're being melodramatic." She wrapped her arms around his neck and inhaled the wonderful soapy fragrance of the skin on his shoulder.

"Probably." He covered the distance to the bed in a few long strides and lowered her to the mattress, already stripped of the bedspread and blanket.

He'd taken her by surprise in the shower, but this was one man, one woman, and a bed. She still had misgivings, even when she saw the graceful arch of his spine and his delightfully compact backside.

Then he smiled down at her, his eyes dark and challenging, his face softened with passion. She loved him. There was no turning back. She found the courage to reach out to him.

She raised her arms, and he came down between them, hovering over her while he mesmerized her with his eyes.

"You're exquisite," he said quietly, taking her chin in his hand and barely brushing her lips with his. "I want to make you wonderfully happy."

"You are." She pulled him down, cradling his cheek against her breast, feeling protective, loving, and deliciously aroused all at the same time.

Max wanted to ask questions of her. Has any man touched you like this? Have you ever felt this way before? He was a stranger to himself at this moment, jealous even of that fool on the television who'd claimed to have kissed her when they were adolescents.

Ordinarily he had little sexual curiosity about the women he bedded. He assumed they were experienced and wouldn't want them to be otherwise.

Leigh was turning all his liberal ideas upside down. He wanted to be the first to introduce her to lovemaking. It had nothing to do with the sexual act as he'd always performed it and everything to do with her mysterious attraction.

At this moment nothing mattered but being with

her. He wanted to hold her in his arms forever. He was intoxicated by the scent of her skin and enraptured by the depths of her hazel eyes. Her laughter was more pleasing than the finest symphony, her lips more beautiful than a rose garden in bloom.

He rolled onto his side and rested his hand on the swell of her creamy white hip, lowering his head to her breast. Suckling gently, he heard a purr of contentment deep in her throat and moved his hand lower to rest between her thighs.

"You're lovely. So lovely." The impact of her beauty overwhelmed him. He couldn't stop telling her.

Stretching his length beside her, he pulled her against his torso, locking her there with his arm and leg. Oddly, his raging need subsided. He was still hard and throbbing, but he was wholly in control, wanting to prolong the joy of discovery as long as possible.

She snuggled against him, tentatively teasing his nipple with the tip of her tongue, creating spasms of pleasure that rippled through him with electrifying tension. He explored her pleasure points with his hands and mouth and tried to suppress the growing intensity of his own need. She moaned seductively when he massaged her back from her neck to her ankles, showering her with kisses.

"Please, Max, oh, please..."

She rolled onto her back and reached for him, pulling him closer with more strength than he'd dreamed of finding in her slim, shapely arms. Their lips met as her legs circled his hips and he entered her.

Nothing was this good; nothing felt this wonderful. Every nerve in her being was vibrating from his rhythmic movements. His lips set her skin afire; his hands made her delirious with pleasure. He filled her with sensations that kept building with every stroke. She heard breathless cries and belatedly realized they were her own.

He cried out, too, and she recognized her name, but the rest of the words spilling from his heart and his mouth were foreign. The whole world was rocking, and he was with her. He was part of her. It was going to happen. Max was going to make it happen.

"Oh, Max!" There were no words for what was building inside her. "Oh!"

She arched her back to meet his final thrust, and he held her suspended between two dimensions, her legs trembling as wave after wave of pure pleasure swept through her.

"I didn't know..." she said, more to herself than him.

Tenderly, he pulled up the sheet before he stretched out beside her, cradling her against his chest.

"I've never... Not like that."

"Never?"

"It was..." She was so sleepy she was afraid she might be dreaming.

"It's never been so wonderful for me," he whispered into her ear.

"It makes everything else seem like a waste of time." Her eyes drifted shut, and she snuggled closer to him.

When she awoke the only light was from the small lamp on the bedside table. Max was still beside her, watching her, his face still softened with passion.

"Can it happen again?" she wondered aloud.

"Again and again and again, sweetheart."

"You didn't harrumph, not once all evening," she remembered, still in a happy daze.

"Then I must name your penalty. One hundred kisses, payable beginning now."

"You're a tyrant!"

She always paid her debts, but by the time the light of dawn crept in around the edges of the curtain, he had a mortgage on her soul.

## ❧ 11 ☙

**B**right sun streamed into the room, and the rich aroma of coffee was almost enough to coax Leigh out of bed.

She rolled onto her back and stretched lazily, too content to worry about the time.

"Good morning, darling." His accent was more pronounced than usual, making his voice deliciously sexy.

"Oh, you're up."

Not only was Max wide awake, he was dressed. She got one glimpse of his superbly tailored Italian suit and pulled the sheet over her head.

"Go away. Please. I'm not ready for morning."

"I brought you some coffee."

"That's sweet of you. Please leave it on the nightstand."

"Very well, but I want to kiss you good morning."

"You did that hours ago."

"So I did. Then let me kiss you good noonday. I have to leave for a luncheon meeting."

She felt the bed move when he sat down beside her, then he started to pull the sheet away, beginning at the bottom. When cool air hit her toes, she gave up, pushing herself to a sitting position and clutching the sheet to her breasts.

"This isn't fair. You're all clean and combed and..."

Shaved, she thought, feeling his smooth chin against hers as he covered her mouth for a long lingering kiss. Her lips were so tender it was like walking over pebbles in shallow water: uncomfortable but too much fun to stop.

"I don't want to leave you," he said, cupping her chin and looking into her eyes. "But we depart for Miami this afternoon, and I must confer with some people."

"I'll miss you."

Was it a mistake to admit it? She was beyond caring.

"A pair of keycards for your room are on the dresser. I insisted they recode the lock since your card was stolen. Albert drew a hot bath for you here and brought a small selection of fresh clothing—"

"Albert came in here?"

"Yes, he just left."

"He saw me sleeping in your bed?"

"Don't be concerned. There's no possibility Albert will ever write a royal expose. He comes from a distinguished line of gentlemen's gentlemen. Discretion is bred into him."

"Still, you should have warned me so I could leave before he came. I'm embarrassed that he saw me."

"My rights to privacy were taken away the moment I left my mother's womb. You're making too much of this. Albert has duties to perform, among them waking me in the morning."

"I don't care what your valet does for you. I don't want to be watched while I'm sleeping."

"Then I owe you an apology," he said stiffly. "I derived a great deal of pleasure observing you while you slept." He stood and walked toward the door.

"It's not the same thing, Max, and you know it."

"No, it isn't," he said crossly, leaving without a goodbye.

This was no way to begin the day after. She wanted to call him back and tell him how wonderful he was. She needed to hear soft loving words in the light of day, needed to know whether their love-making was as special to him as it was to her.

For several long minutes she stared at the closed

door, hoping he'd come back if only to say, "See you later."

"Another day, another city," she said aloud, forcing herself to get up, then trailing the king-size sheet across the room to the window because it felt too weird to walk around naked in a prince's bedroom that was frequented by his valet.

The best thing about last night—or at least one of the really good things—was that she'd forgotten for a while that Max was really Prince Maximilian.

She peeked out the side of the curtain and squinted against the bright sunlight. The trip was winding down and so was their ill-conceived engagement. She was only beginning to accept how complicated it would be explaining things to everyone she knew—and to a lot of nosy reporters she didn't want to know.

She trudged toward the tub of hot water, wishing she could turn back the clock. Her life had been so pleasantly uncomplicated before she fell in love.

Max's day went badly from the time he left the hotel. One of the key investors had to cancel out of the luncheon due to a family crisis.

The meal was catered in the bank's boardroom,

and Max set his mouth on fire with some innocent-looking seafood sauce, then scorched his tongue for real when he gulped his too-hot coffee to wash away the burning sensation.

He provided amusement for the Texans, only to learn they were unwilling to make a decision without the absent financier. They promised to email an answer to him later in the week, but he regretted the time wasted—time that could have been spent with Leigh.

Hans drove him directly from the meeting to the airport, where he found the plane had already boarded and was scheduled to leave momentarily for Atlanta—where they would change planes for Miami.

Worse, it was overbooked, and he'd been treated as a no-show, doubtless in spite of Albert's vehement protests. His seat and Hans' were occupied by an outspoken couple who resented having to give up first-class accommodations they hadn't paid for. They fussed loudly until the flight attendants finally coaxed an elderly couple to relinquish their seats in the rear in return for valuable vouchers.

Leigh was sitting by a window, the aisle seat beside her occupied by a giant of a man with the look of a professional football player. She nodded once at Max, then appeared to be absorbed in a paperback novel.

Max had counted on changing places with either Albert or Fred when he'd finished discussing business matters with Hans—if she'd chosen to sit by one of them—and it irked him that he couldn't get close to her. Nor did her cool attitude encourage him to suggest she change seats with Hans.

Even though he'd been running late for his meeting, he shouldn't have left her so abruptly. He'd been insensitive about Albert.

He should have realized it would embarrass her to have his valet moving about the room while she was still in bed. He tried to catch her eye again while he waited awkwardly to be seated, but she kept hers glued on the pages of the book. He'd have to wait until they changed planes in Atlanta to speak to her.

He wanted to kick himself for not chartering a small plane. Usually he enjoyed the bustle of foreign airports and the relative comfort of first-class accommodations, but today everything that kept him apart from Leigh was an annoyance.

She could feel his eyes on her. She turned pages without trying to read them but refused to look up until she was sure Max was seated several rows ahead.

What could they possibly talk about on a crowded plane?

What was left to be said, no matter where they talked? Miami loomed ahead like a black hole. He'd jet home to his palace and forget all about her. She'd try to salvage her career and her self-respect. It was a total downer to realize no one, especially not Max, would ever know she was willing to paddle a canoe across the ocean if that was what it took to stay with him.

Isn't that a big joke, Your Royal Highness? she silently asked him.

When the plane landed in Atlanta, he stayed in his seat until she walked past, then inserted himself into the line of passengers inching toward the exit.

"I wanted to sit by you," he said, grasping the equipment bag she still didn't trust to airline baggage handlers. "You really should let Fred take care of this."

"I'm not asking you to carry it. I'm perfectly capable of carrying my own bag."

She tried to take it back just as the flight attendant was giving Max her sunniest goodbye smile. He held it tightly as they squeezed through the plane door, more or less together, and resisted another tug as they walked up the exit ramp.

"Leigh, darling, are you trying to embarrass me?" he asked.

"Carry it, then." His teasing tone annoyed her. "And I'm not your darling."

"I want to apologize for—"

She glanced up and saw his bodyguards well within sight—and hearing.

"Don't you dare!" she said under her breath, dashing ahead—in the wrong direction.

Fred cut her off after a few hundred feet of dodging travelers who were streaming toward the main concourse.

"Please, miss, this way," he said urgently, probably petrified his career would go down the tubes if he lost her.

His Highness didn't deign to run after her himself.

They made the connection with no time to spare. She couldn't stop Max from sitting beside her, but he was so quiet even a harrumph would have been welcome.

After a half hour that seemed two days long, he spoke without looking at her.

"I only wanted to express my regrets for letting Albert into the room. It was insensitive, and I hope you'll accept my apology."

A harrumph would have sounded friendlier.

"I thought you were going to apologize for... I misunderstood."

"Should I be sorry for...other things?"

"No, of course not!" She bit her lip. "I'm planning to stay in my own apartment tonight. Since I live in the city, a hotel room really isn't necessary."

"We're invited to a party at the hotel this evening. It would be more convenient if you'd stay there. I've already arranged for your accommodations. It would simplify the arrangements."

"About tonight, I really think I'll pass. You can tell your guests I'm sick or something."

"It will be very awkward if you're not there. Surely, you're not going to let me down."

"You really don't need me."

"Let me be the judge of that. I'm holding you to our agreement."

"Our agreement," she repeated dismally.

The old Leigh would've put up a fight, but instead, she gave in and hated herself for having the backbone of a worm. She'd go to his party, but only because it was easier to put off their final farewell than to deal with it now.

She glanced at his profile. Strong features like his belonged on a postage stamp, not on a snapshot tucked away in her billfold. He was major league; she was sandlot.

She closed her eyes and pretended to sleep.

Tonight would be different, she learned from Max on the way to the grandiose pseudo-Spanish hotel, probably the poshest in South Florida. The party wasn't business. An old school friend of Max's had flown in from the Bahamas and was throwing a reunion bash. A hundred or so of their best friends would be there.

"Would this be a good time to break off our engagement?" she asked, dreading the curiosity and congratulations of people who cared about Max as a person.

"It would be a terrible time. I need you as my fiancée more tonight than at any other event on the schedule. Please tell me you're not serious."

She *was* serious, but when Max targeted her with his intense dark eyes, she didn't have the energy to deny him.

"Oh, all right. I'll play my part for one more party."

She wasn't being gracious in defeat, but Max didn't seem to notice. He busied himself with a newspaper as soon as she agreed not to deviate from the itinerary: ***Prince Escorts Fiancée to Evening Party.***

She was booked into a suite at this hotel, but by the time she was registered and had accounted for all her luggage, there wasn't time to enjoy the spacious rooms. She took one look at the machine-carved imitations of Spanish colonial furniture and rushed off to the hotel salon to be made presentable.

Albert, of course, had made the appointment. She still hadn't managed to look him in the eye.

She should've looked great when she got back from the salon. Her hair was piled high in elegant coils so she could wear the collar of imitation pearls that went with the floor-length black column gown, the last unworn outfit in her temporary wardrobe. Her makeup was skillfully applied, masking the fatigue shadowing her eyes, but cosmetics couldn't conceal the misery there or the unhappy cast of her mouth. After she dressed, she practiced looking happy in the mirror, but it was no go. Max should have hired an actress to play his fiancée.

In spite of her misgivings, her heart leaped when she heard the knock. Even if Max chose to be cold or aloof this evening, she suffered less in his presence than away from him.

Was she going to turn into a batty old lady, her apartment walls covered with clippings about the prince who got away?

She opened the door, prepared to smile gamely and go to the party.

"Good evening, miss," Hans said. "His Highness

requested that I give these to you." He handed her a familiar key chain with a battered alligator emblem. It was the one her brother had given her years before when she'd passed the driving test for her license.

"Your vehicle is in the parking garage. Here's your claim check."

"Thank you."

She wanted to cry. Now that she had transportation, there was absolutely no reason not to go home in the morning.

"His Highness requests that you join him at the cocktail party on the mezzanine. If you'll allow me?" He offered his arm with a boyish grin.

"It would be my pleasure."

She tossed the keys on the bed and left with the bodyguard.

The party didn't start for Max until he saw Leigh arrive. Perhaps he shouldn't have delegated the privilege of escorting her to Hans, but he didn't trust himself alone with her in a room with a bed. The aching void he felt whenever she was out of his sight should have lessened after he'd made love to her. He'd been insatiable, hoping familiarity would diminish his need, but the opposite had happened.

He wanted her so badly he resented it, but more than ever, he loathed the idea of letting her interview him. Her article would be worse than appearing nude on the cover of the sleaziest tabloid. It would be a betrayal of what he felt for her.

His friend, Peter Mills, was telling him an involved story, leading up to one of the punch lines that had earned him the label of class clown when they'd been boys together in a Swiss boarding school. Max tried to concentrate, but when Leigh stepped off the elevator on Hans' arm, he totally lost the thread of his friend's tale.

"Here's my fiancée," he interrupted, then realized he hated lying to someone who knew him as well as Peter did.

More than that, he detested the lie itself. What had possessed him to involve this lovely young woman in a foolish ruse? He could only imagine how tumultuous her life would be after the engagement was formally terminated. Would the boost to her career be worth the misery—hers and his?

Peter whistled through his teeth. "Wow! What a looker!"

Max disliked the compliment, even though he knew his reaction was irrational. It was only natural for other men to be stunned by her beauty. He was totally under its spell and half out of his mind wanting her, but he'd sworn to stay away from her after this party.

He didn't want to marry a woman who was using him to advance her career, so there was no future in their relationship. He cared about her too deeply to make her his mistress—especially when his father was expecting him to return home with the matter of his marriage settled.

She saw him and started walking toward him, but a knot of people moved between them.

"Max, it's so good to see you." Natasha rushed toward him, linking her arm with his, overwhelming his senses with the heady scent of jasmine. "I can't tell you how often I've regretted the hurricane that kept you from meeting me."

"It was fate, Natasha." He shrugged without managing to loosen her grip on his arm. "Are you here with the man from Chicago—what was his name?"

Her laugher trilled; he suspected she practiced it.

"Good heavens, no! He was only a casual acquaintance. You know perfectly well I followed you to Chicago in case things didn't work out with your fiancée. Where is she, by the way? Have you broken her heart the way you do with all women?"

"Certainly not." He could feel the bite of her fingernails through the sleeve of his tux. She wasn't going to be easy to lose, but he tried to conceal his impatience. He owed her a measure of courtesy after failing to reschedule their assignation.

He looked urgently toward the elevators, but Leigh had disappeared from sight.

Peter succeeded where he'd failed. He detached Natasha from Max's arm.

"Aren't you going to introduce me to this lovely creature, Max?"

"Certainly. Peter, this is Natasha. Natasha, Peter Mills, our host."

"Mr. Mills, will you forgive me for crashing your party? A friend insisted..."

Max hurried away, hoping his twice-divorced-but-now-single friend would be interested enough to keep Natasha occupied.

"Hans!" He saw the bodyguard and barked out his name with unintentional harshness; he was angry at himself, not this man.

"Your Highness, Miss Bailey was with me just a moment ago. I think she must have gone down the stairs. I don't see her anywhere on this level."

He pointed at the green-and-gold carpeted stairway leading to the ground floor.

"Watch for her here," Max ordered brusquely.

He went down the stairs two at a time, worried she might leave now that her car was available at the hotel. He couldn't force her to stay, but he didn't want to think about that as he rushed through the lobby, looking in every direction.

He found her by the replica of a suit of armor; rather, he spotted her backing around it, pursued by an aggressive-looking man. He wore a charcoal-gray suit and tasseled loafers with white socks. He was gesturing energetically but didn't seem to be making sexual overtures. Max moved closer, taking care not to be seen by Leigh.

"I'm not talking out of the side of my mouth, Miss Bailey. The head editor gave me that figure—a cool half million advance, and they want the book yesterday. If you need help writing it, they'll get someone for you."

"I am not writing a book about the prince. Not yesterday, not tomorrow!"

"With me as your agent, the book offer is only the tip of the iceberg. I'll be talking to TV, and I can wrap up a deal with *Sensations* magazine that'll buy you a sports car with mink upholstery."

"The only animal I'd like skinned is you! Hear this. I will not pose nude for a girlie magazine. I will not write a book about Prince Maximilian. And the North Pole will melt before I let you represent me. Have I said anything you don't understand?"

"If it's the money, I can do better. The half mil was only a feeler. If you marry this prince—"

"I'm calling hotel security."

Max smiled ruefully. The lady certainly could take care of herself, but he'd never had a stronger urge to create some mayhem.

He came up behind the little weasel and grabbed the back of his jacket and the belt holding up his trousers.

"Hotel security," he said gruffly, winking at Leigh behind the man's back. "We can't allow our guests to be harassed."

"I wasn't harassing! You got no right— Let go or I'll sue!"

Max half dragged and half carried the blustering agent across the lobby, stopping in front of a pool below an artificial waterfall. The man squealed loudly when Max hefted him over the tiled rim and plopped him in the shallow water.

"You'll hear from my lawyer," the agent screamed. "I'll put this hotel out of business."

"Don't bother calling him," Max said with a grin of satisfaction. "I have nothing to do with the hotel, but I do have diplomatic immunity. The only question is whether Miss Bailey wishes to press charges against *you*."

He turned his back and walked briskly over to Leigh, offering his arm.

"The party is upstairs. I suggest we both join it."

She'd laughed when the overbearing agent landed in the pool, but one look at Max's face squelched her good humor. She saw thunderclouds hovering around him and wondered if he thought she'd done something to encourage the man.

"I didn't come down to meet him, if that's what you're thinking. I'd never seen the man before," she said, hard-pressed to keep up with the long skirt impeding her stride. "Anyway, I had the situation under control. I told him to leave me alone."

"From where I stood, he didn't appear to be listening," Max said without any sign of agitation.

He acted as though tossing people into pools was an everyday occurrence. Maybe it was in his genes—a royal talent for punishing wrongdoers.

"Anyway, I can take care of myself," she said.

If he went in for rescuing damsels in distress, she thought, he could at least be a little more cheerful about it.

The cocktail party was breaking up. The guests were slowly making their way to the private room where dinner would be served. Apparently, the guest of honor had been missed. He was virtually swamped by admirers as soon as he set foot on the mezzanine.

It was a long evening. Only sheer exhaustion and

a vague hope that Max might yet come to her room kept Leigh from claiming her car and driving home at three in the morning.

Were any of the dazzling, clever, rich women who were at the party in the running as a bride for the prince?

She sat in bed torturing herself by trying to remember all the women he'd danced with after dinner—the lead of a television series, an opera star on her way to Milan, a woman whose family name was a household word for cleaning products.

He hadn't used her to ward off would-be brides at Peter's party. In fact, he seemed to welcome the attention of every female in attendance. He only danced with her twice, and that seemed like two times too many if his mood was any indication.

As soon as she had a few hours' sleep, she was going home.

## ❧ 1 2 ❧

His palms were moist, his mouth like cotton. Max rubbed his eyes, trying to get rid of the gritty feeling caused by lack of sleep.

He felt conspicuous standing outside Leigh's door, but he still wasn't sure what to say to her. He should apologize for his abominable behavior at the party last night, but what he really wanted was to explain the torment he'd suffered by not dancing every dance with her. He'd deliberately deprived himself of her company, trying to put her out of his mind by showering attention on other women. He'd failed miserably. Watching her in the arms of other men was sheer torture.

How could he return to his old life without her? What choice did he have? Even if he could convince his father and his people that she was a suitable princess, how could he convince himself?

He doubted her feelings for him went much beyond an avid interest in writing about him. With every aspect of his life constantly scrutinized by the press, he couldn't bring himself to make a public spectacle of his love life. He dreaded the kind of kiss-and-tell article she might possibly write.

For self-preservation, he should walk away without speaking to her.

She was behind that door, perhaps still curled up under the covers, her lashes feathery long on delicate lids. He imagined the fineness of her features and the sleek smoothness of her skin. He wanted to cradle his cheek between her breasts and feel the silky softness of her hair spilling over his arm.

Or perhaps she was bathing, pink and moist, ready to be wrapped in a towel. He loved every part of her—slender arms and gracefully molded shoulders, her queenly carriage with head proudly erect on the beautiful column of her neck. He ached remembering the collar of pearls she'd worn so successfully at the party.

He wanted to adorn her naked body with his family's jewels: the diamond tiara, sapphires and diamonds for her earlobes, a long strand of pearls caressing her beautiful breasts, a fire opal in her navel. He could cover her arms with precious bangles and bracelets and wrap her shapely ankles with chains of gold. But no embellishments could make her lovelier than she already was in his eyes.

He was paralyzed by alien feelings—shyness, nervousness, fear of making a mistake. In his entire life he'd never been intimidated by anyone, except perhaps his father when he was very young and mischievous. It was incredible that this beautiful American was turning his own image of himself upside down.

With bittersweet determination, he raised his hand and knocked softly on her door.

He counted slowly to thirty, giving her adequate time to respond before he knocked again, then rapped loudly three times to wake her if she was still sleeping.

Had she left? His stomach knotted in anxiety.

He believed in fate. A man could no more control his destiny than he could move the earth from its axis. A few words printed on a bumper sticker had changed his life. Even if he walked away at this moment and flew home without ever seeing Leigh again, he would never forget her.

He'd never been passionately in love before, and he probably never would be again.

Stunned by his admission, he stared at the closed

door and saw even more clearly why he couldn't ask Leigh to be his wife. He'd always seen himself as a risk taker, a man with the courage to lead his country in the twenty-first century. In truth, he was a coward, afraid to offer his love to a woman who might use it without returning it.

He turned to leave just as the door opened.

"Max, I wasn't expecting you."

She was fully dressed, wearing casual tan trousers and a tailored navy blouse open at the throat—her own clothing, simple ready-mades she wore as successfully as the stylish evening gowns.

"I thought perhaps you were— But that doesn't matter."

"Do you want to come in?"

He noticed a housekeeping cart less than six doors away and nodded his head, struck dumb by the impact she had on him. Her hair was loose, spilling over her shoulders in disarray, and the brush in her hand told him she was in the process of arranging it.

He stepped inside and closed the door, reaching out like a man in a trance and taking the brush from her unresisting hand.

He didn't ask, and she didn't protest. He moved behind her and began brushing her hair, the silence between them broken only by crackles of static electricity. The ends of her locks danced under the strokes of the brush, then he abandoned it, running his fingers through her hair.

"Your hair is beautiful," he said, speaking for the first time.

"Is that why you came—to tell me that?"

She turned and faced him, and he was pleased that her face was free of makeup. Her lips were rose-petal pink, and he desperately wanted to feel them on his body. He reached out and touched them with the tips of his fingers, but she didn't respond, didn't part her pearly white teeth and caress his fingers with the tip of her tongue.

"Maybe you shouldn't have come," she whispered hoarsely, lifting his hand and setting it at his side.

"I'm sorry."

"No. I don't want you to be sorry. You do exactly as you please, then you expect me to be thrilled by your apologies."

"That's not the way it is." He felt as though he'd been slapped.

"Then tell me. For what, exactly, are you apologizing? For insisting I go to a party? Your reason for that escapes me."

"We did have an agreement."

"Yes, but I don't know why anymore. You certainly don't object to being pursued by women."

"That's not true. I only fulfilled my social obligations by dancing with the guests at Peter's party." He felt cornered, and lies came much more easily than the truth.

"I'm much too busy to listen to fairy tales."

She walked over to the bed where she'd arranged piles of clothing in an order that escaped him.

"I imagine Albert will be the one to haul all this to the thrift shop. I've put the things that need laundering in that plastic bag. I've never given away designer clothes before, so I don't know about having them cleaned first."

"I wish you'd keep them. The silver gown—"

"—would look silly at the office Christmas party."

"Then at least keep the suits. Surely a career woman can use them," he said, angry at her for being stubborn—and at himself for so badly botching what was supposed to be an apology.

"Stop it, Max! Or should I say Your Highness now that our engagement is over?"

"Is it over?" he asked bleakly. "Have you made the announcement to the press?"

"No, I'm not going to."

For one instant he misinterpreted what she said, allowing himself to hope she didn't want their engagement to end. But of course, her main concern was the interview, the cozy chat he'd promised. He was honor-bound to go through with it, even though it would be agonizing. How could he bare his soul to this...this reporter without revealing the love that was tearing him apart?

"How do you want it handled?" he asked.

"It's in your hands. I won't be talking to the press about our breakup or anything else."

She fussed with the clothing on the bed, smoothing a skirt, buttoning a jacket, and picking up a jewelry box to look at the collar of imitation pearls.

Upset as he was, he still longed to see real pearls against her fair skin. He was tormented by a vision of her body adorned with only precious jewels.

He walked over to the window and spoke with his back to her, unwilling to let her see how aroused he was.

Would she resist if he tried to make love to her again? His need for her was so intense he nearly dropped to his knees at her feet and confessed all that was in his heart. He could bear the humiliation, but not the possibility she might reject him. He cursed his stiff-necked pride and regretted the day he'd met her, then tried to concentrate on ending the fiasco of their engagement with as little public clamor as possible.

"When I arrive home, I'll make a small announcement for our press. Does it suit you if I say it was a mutual decision with no negative feelings on either side?"

"Whatever you like."

He would have preferred an argument; after all, he had promised to let her be the one to break it off.

"If you prefer, I can say it was your decision. Or you can make the announcement..."

"Max, it doesn't matter. No one cares what I do— the world is only interested in you. Say or do whatever is easiest for you."

"I'll give it some thought, but I promise not to embarrass you in any way."

"Thank you."

Her voice was listless, and she kept fidgeting with the garments on the bed. He wanted to take her in his arms, but what could he say to a woman who was getting exactly what she wanted—an exclusive story for her magazine?

"Where are you going now?" He didn't want to hear the answer, but he lacked the will to walk out of the room.

"Home."

"And then to your office?"

"Not today. I'm on vacation. I've accumulated about three weeks' time off, so I may not go in next week, either."

"I see." He didn't, but her job was the last thing

he wanted to discuss. "Then all we have to do is get on with your interview. Would you like to do it now?"

"No." She'd been expecting him to mention it, but she wasn't anywhere near ready to deal with him as the subject of an article. "I mean, I have some work to do first—a question outline, a little research. How much longer will you be here?"

She braced herself, expecting him to say he'd be leaving in a day or two.

"I have to spend a few days in Washington before I can leave. I really do have a few chores to perform as a representative of Schwanstein."

"Well, pick a time that's convenient for you. Any day but today."

She wasn't sure putting it off was a good idea. She could do the interview anytime. The tape recorder was ready, and she'd jotted down enough questions to write a book. The longer she waited, the more she'd dread it.

"May I call you after I've checked my appointment calendar?" he asked in the formal tone that reminded her of his lofty status.

"Fine."

"If you're not going to your office today, could I trouble you for your phone number?'

"I could call you— No, I'll give it to you. Let me find some paper."

How could this be a five-star hotel when they didn't provide a notepad? Or was she half-blind from the tears she wouldn't let surface?

This wasn't a real breakup, but it sure felt like one. Consider the facts—he had ignored her at the party last night and hadn't come to her room afterward. If that didn't add up to being dumped, she'd rather not wait around for the final act in his little farce.

She dug into her purse and found a letter she'd addressed to her mother explaining her pretend engagement. She'd written it instead of calling or texting because she could sort through her feelings much better with pen and paper. She'd never mailed it, so she extracted the letter and used the envelope to jot down her number.

"About last evening," he said. "I'm afraid you didn't enjoy yourself."

"Of course I did. Your friend Peter is delightful. He has a wonderful sense of humor. We must have danced a dozen times."

She was trilling like that dope, Natasha, but anything was better than admitting how hurt she'd been when Max scarcely paid any attention to her.

"So I noticed," he said in a sour tone that gave her an instant of hope—which was dashed when he reminded her of the incident with the agent. "I'm sorry you were bothered by that man in the lobby."

She shrugged. "I didn't need rescuing, but I have to say you did it with flair."

"He's a parasite. I hope he won't try to contact you again. I don't think he's the kind of person to entrust with your career."

"I won't be posing nude, if you're worried about it."

"I never thought you would."

He was dressed casually—for him—in a navy blazer and dove-gray slacks. He wasn't even wearing a tie, and the first button on his polo shirt was open, revealing a few dark hairs on his chest. She was having a hard time believing she'd lain in his arms, her cheek caressed by those silky hairs, her knee tucked between his legs, feeling the softness and the hardness of him.

She turned her back, afraid he'd see the pain and longing in her eyes. If knowing Max had taught her anything, it had to be that she wasn't an actress. She wasn't good at pretending to be his fiancée, and she was at a loss when it came to concealing her love for him.

She tried to think of things she really hated about him so she wouldn't break down. The worst thing she could do was blubber about how much she loved him.

Obviously, their lovemaking had meant little to him. He hadn't even tried to be with her again.

There wasn't anything about him to hate. He was a prince and a gentleman. Dancing with other women had been his way of showing her there was nothing substantial between them. Maybe he felt guilty for seducing her, but face it, she'd been easy. Even now, hurting as she did, she was ready to fall into his arms if he gave any indication of wanting her.

She entertained a fantasy of making love on top of all the designer clothes. She wanted to spread the silver dress under her and hug him and kiss him and squeeze him until he wanted her more than any man had ever wanted a woman.

Instead, she took one last look at her luxurious suite, hoisted her two bags and purse onto her shoulders, and announced, "I'm ready to leave."

"Let me help you," he offered politely.

"No! I mean no, thank you. I'm used to managing on my own. I'll be just fine."

"You're a stubborn female, Leigh Bailey. Would it be so terrible if I carried your luggage to your car?"

"Not terrible, no," she said thoughtfully, knowing she couldn't tell him the real reason for rejecting his help. She couldn't bear to be with this polite stranger a moment longer.

Leaving him was the hardest thing she'd ever had

to do, but she wanted to say goodbye with class. No tears or hysterics for this girl. She wouldn't throw her arms around his neck and cling to him. She wouldn't put him on the spot by kissing him as no man had ever been kissed.

"I'd like to leave now, Max. I'd rather go alone."

His eyes were hooded, his expression unreadable.

"Wait," he said.

She froze, rooted by an involuntary rush of hope. He couldn't let her walk away. He had to see they were made for each other.

His words quickly brought her back to the real world.

"I want very much to give you a gift. Will you accept this?" He held out the jeweler's box with the collar. "I only wish they were real pearls."

"Max, I..." Something inside her died. It didn't matter whether the choker went to a thrift shop or lay in her drawer for the rest of her life. She'd never wear it again; it certainly didn't evoke happy memories.

She managed to thank him as though she meant it. Her mother would have been proud; she'd been well taught as a child. She stuffed the box into her bag beside the camera and left him standing in the middle of the room.

Leigh claimed her car and drove home in a fog of misery, certain she was leaving behind the best part of her life.

Her apartment had the dank, deserted atmosphere of a place that had been empty for years. She blamed it on the humidity but suspected the gloom originated in her head. Cinderella must have felt the same way when she went back to the home of her wretched stepmother after the ball.

She had kept to her agreement to not use her cell phone while they were pretend engaged. Now that it was over, it was time to face the real world. Her voicemail was flashing with the urgency of a four-alarm fire. She started listening to messages.

"Bailey, call me as soon as you can."

At least half were from her editor, but she was too depressed to open that can of worms by calling him.

The last message was the only one that surprised her.

"Leigh, my calendar is clear tomorrow afternoon. If you would like to interview me at the hotel, I'll be in my room at three o'clock. If this isn't satisfactory, please call me."

Max gave a number, but she erased it along with

all her other messages. She wished her memories of the prince could be eradicated so easily.

She woke up the next morning grimly determined to put Prince Maximilian behind her. It hurt. Oh, how it hurt! But what were her choices? She could delude herself into thinking something good might come of interviewing him—or she could face reality. Princes didn't fall in love with female reporters.

Max loathed the attention he got from the tabloids, and he didn't rate *Celebrity* magazine any higher than the sleaziest rag. He would hate anything she wrote, and she'd hate herself for writing it.

She couldn't do the article.

Anything she wrote would be a mockery of what she felt for him. She couldn't get past her emotions; she especially couldn't exploit him for the sake of a pat on the back from Ed Waverly or a chance at a job she no longer wanted.

There was no way she could interview Max, not even if her career depended on it—and it probably did.

Waverly would freak out. He was counting on a juicy expose, and he'd be getting zilch. Her only decision was whether to resign or let him fire her.

Pride urged her to quit, but her finances suggested it might be better to get kicked out and collect unemployment while she job-hunted.

What could a reporter do when she lost her edge? Even a job at a car wash would be better than a kiss-and-tell article: ***How I Slept with a Prince*** or ***The Case of the Mangled Heart***.

The polite thing to do was phone and cancel the interview, but she couldn't do it. She felt sick to her stomach every time she tried to pick up the phone.

Max canceled his lunch with Peter and worked out in the hotel fitness center until he'd expended his last ounce of energy. Then he showered, dressed, and waited.

With an hour to go before Leigh was due, he made sure they wouldn't be interrupted by any of his men, then went over dozens of possible questions in his head.

"Tell me, Your Highness," he mimicked aloud, "what are your marriage plans? I understand Schwanstein needs an heir or the country becomes part of Austria."

He didn't have an answer to that one. In fact, he was woefully inarticulate when it came to responding to any question of importance. It was as though his life was on hold. He was burning up with anticipation but too confused to make plans.

Three o'clock came and went.

She was late.

At four, he called her. She didn't pick up the phone. He left a terse but polite message.

At four thirty, his message was less courteous; at five, he was wildly impatient.

"Leigh, please call me immediately. This interview has to be done today. I can be available this evening if that's more convenient, and I'll meet you anywhere you choose."

He regretted every word the instant he hung up. What he wanted to say to her couldn't be left on a voicemail. He picked up the envelope again. There, in the upper left-hand corner, she'd printed the return address—her address—in neat block letters: The El Camino Apartments, Number Forty-Two.

Leigh went through the motions of going to bed. She brushed her hair and teeth, put on her sleep shirt, and crawled between sheets she'd just laundered.

She even flipped on the small TV on her dresser

and channel surfed until all the images on the screen began to look the same.

She was playing a losing game.

Instead of going away, her sense of loss kept growing. Nothing in her ordinary routine was comforting. She couldn't bring herself to call friends or seek out their companionship.

She got up and replayed Max's messages, knowing she should erase them. It hurt to hear his voice over and over, but the thought of never hearing it again was worse.

The last thing she expected was a summons from the intercom in the lobby. Someone wanted to come up to her apartment, not exactly a soothing prospect for a woman living alone. Her caller buzzed again and again, and she had visions of her editor down below with handcuffs to chain her to her desk until she produced the article he wanted.

She pressed her intercom button. "Who is it?" she asked, trying to sound groggy with sleep in case she wanted to get rid of her midnight caller.

"Max. May I come up, please?"

It was an order, not a request. She didn't even consider refusing.

He was wearing the suede jacket with tight black jeans and a silk shirt so white it gleamed in the dim light from the single floor lamp in her living room.

She saw her geometric-patterned couch and light oak tables through his eyes, but it didn't matter if he liked her taste.

"Why didn't you come for the interview?" he demanded.

She belatedly remembered how revealing her pajamas were and folded her arms across her chest.

"I didn't want to interview you. There won't be an article."

He didn't say anything. Instead, he stared at her, his eyes blazing with strong emotion.

"I can't write it," she said defensively. "I'm sorry if you're disappointed."

"Disappointed?" He sounded incredulous.

"Oh, go away! I can't write the article or anything else. I never will. Now leave me alone!"

"No, Leigh, that's exactly what I'm not going to do. Come with me."

"Where? Why?"

"Next you'll ask me who, what, when, and how. Isn't that the formula reporters follow?"

"I'm probably not a reporter anymore, but that's not your concern. What are you doing?"

He'd located the coat closet and found her red rain poncho.

"Getting your coat."

"I'm not going anywhere."

"Trust me, you are."

He dropped the poncho over her head and gave her no choice but to stuff her arms through the holes.

"Max, are you crazy? What—"

"Where are your shoes? Never mind, I'll find a pair."

He disappeared into her bedroom and came back with her best black pumps, three-inch heels with delicate straps.

Max dropped to his knees and lifted first one foot, then the other, sliding the shoes over her bare toes. She didn't know whether to laugh, cry, or hug him.

He gave her just enough time to snatch her purse and hope her apartment key was in it, then he propelled her down the stairs and through the entryway.

The parking lot was well lit, so it didn't take a full moon to spot his transportation: a white stretch limo with, of all things, a sticker on the rear bumper.

"What on earth?" She broke free of his hand on her arm and hurried over to read it.

HERE COMES THE BRIDE!

"Here comes the bride?"

"The limo just came back from a wedding. It was all I could get on short notice, and there wasn't time to have it cleaned. If you don't want to sit on rice and confetti, I suggest you ride in front with the driver."

She walked to the front and looked inside through the door he was holding open.

"There isn't a driver."

"Yes, ma'am, there is."

He took her hand, helped her into the front seat, shut the door, and came around to sit behind the wheel.

"Do you know how to drive this?"

"I'm learning."

"Max! Where are you taking me?"

"On a mystery trip." He smiled and wouldn't say any more.

Max drove faster than she liked, but the limo felt as safe as an armored truck. With nothing but oncoming headlights to watch, she became increasingly sleepy. After a while she dozed off.

"Wake up, darling."

"Where are we?"

"See for yourself."

If this was a dream, she didn't want to wake up. The limo had stopped near a weakly flickering sign featuring a grotesque long-legged bird.

"The Pink Flamingo!"

"I'll get the key."

Raindrops splashed against the dark windshield as

he ran into the weirdly familiar office. There couldn't be two places like this in the state of Florida.

He was back in practically no time and eased the big car forward, stopping near the end of the parking area.

"Why are you taking me to the cottage where we waited out the hurricane?"

"Actually, the highway pirate claims that one's occupied. For a small extra charge, he's giving us his best—the honeymoon suite."

"Max, this is insane!"

"Probably."

"What are we doing here?"

"I'm apologizing."

"It's starting to rain harder."

He rushed around to open the door for her, and the dome light showed dark rain spots on the shoulders of his jacket. He was carrying a key attached to a hunk of wood the size of his fist and a plastic shopping bag he'd taken with him into the motel office.

"You'll get your shoes wet," he said.

He scooped her up, giving her no choice but to cling to his neck while he hurried toward a blocky cottage with a dim naked bulb over the door. Somehow, he inserted the key and kicked open the door without dropping her or his sack.

When he flipped on the light switch, she saw that

it really was a suite—if size didn't count. A tiny sitting room had a pair of bamboo chairs with garish fuchsia-and-lime flowers on black cushions.

Max didn't stop there. He bumped the door shut and slid the bolt without putting her down and carried her into the second little room.

"Oh, good grief!" she gasped.

The bed was suspended from the ceiling on brassy chains, and the mirror on the ceiling reflected the whole expanse of a faded pink chenille spread.

"Were you expecting this?" she asked as he put her down on the edge of the bed, which began to undulate gently.

"It exceeds my expectations." He laughed as she scrambled off.

"You kidnapped me in my pajamas and brought me to this...this love nest? When do I hear the why?"

"To apologize."

"It doesn't matter about the party. I don't think this is a good idea."

He took off his jacket and hung it on the back of a wooden straight chair. She stuffed her hands into the pockets of the poncho, showing she had no intention of getting cozy.

"That was the least of my sins, and I was punished by watching you dance with other men."

He sounded sad, regretful. She wanted to put her

arms around him and comfort him, but he was still Prince Maximilian of Schwanstein. A night in a cheap motel wouldn't change that. Or the fact he was leaving her.

"I lied to you. It began here. That's why I felt we had to come back here."

He sat on the edge of the swinging bed and took her hand, drawing her down beside him. They both looked up at the ceiling, then laughed softly.

"I guess it'll hold for one more night," she said, trying to mask her curiosity. She'd never felt so vulnerable. She braced herself, afraid to hear what he was going to say.

"I came to this country in search of a wife."

"But our agreement..."

"...was part of the lie. An excuse to keep you with me."

"All the women you danced with..."

"Prospective brides. Peter was most industrious in gathering a good selection."

"Then you've found someone." How could he be so cruel to bring her here to tell her this?

"Yes, but I don't know if she'll have me."

"No doubt she will. What woman doesn't want to be a princess?"

"I don't want a woman who wants to be a princess. I want a woman who loves me, but I'm

LORI WILDE & & PAM ANDREWS HANSON

afraid my lies and mistrust have destroyed all chance of that."

"Why bring me here? Why tell me this, Max?"

She was on the verge of tears, but she wouldn't let herself break down in front of him.

"I misjudged you. I thought you were only interested in furthering your career."

"No, it was always you." The admission was difficult, but this might be the only chance she'd have to tell him how she felt. "I just wanted to be with you. Who is she? The woman you want to marry?"

"Don't you know?" There was so much warmth and longing in his voice, she almost dared hope.

"But it doesn't make sense. Why pretend we're engaged?"

"Because it was what I wanted more than anything in the world. I fell in love with you during the hurricane, but I couldn't reconcile your profession with the woman I needed as a wife."

"As your wife?"

"I never believed in love at first sight until I saw you standing in the rain, your little car mired down in mud and water dripping off your hair. Or maybe I didn't believe in love at all before then. I was resigned to selecting a wife on the basis of what was good for my country."

He reached out and touched her cheek, his fingertips sliding slowly to her lips and resting there until she lightly kissed them.

"Will you be my wife, Leigh?" he murmured.

"Me? Be your wife?" She'd never believed anything this wonderful could happen to her. "But I'm not princess material."

"All that can be worked through. You'll learn. It's a lot, I know, but I'll be right by your side, coaching you all the way."

She could scarcely breathe. "You mean it?"

"Absolutely, we're a team, you and me. Like Harry and Meghan."

"Oh, Max, I don't know what to say."

"Say yes."

"Are you sure you're prepared for this?"

"I've never been more prepared for anything in my life. I love you. Please say yes."

There were challenges to become a royal, and she wouldn't sweep that under the rug, but the bottom line was that she loved Max. They could work through anything that arose. She believed that with all her heart. "I love you, Max. Yes. Yes, yes, yes!"

One of her shoes fell off, and they both laughed with relief and joy.

"Shall I retrieve it?" he asked.

She flicked her ankle and sent the other shoe flying across the room.

"I think not, but this poncho is really warm."

She dropped from her swinging perch and took it off.

"It won't be easy," he said in a husky voice.

"Being a princess?"

"No, being married to the most beautiful woman in the world. I'll have to guard against becoming jealous of every man who smiles at you."

"Max, do you really want to marry me?"

"On my honor."

"I'll get old and gray. Will you love me then?"

"Your real beauty is inside. I've known that from the beginning. There is a custom in my family—to give a love token to seal royal engagements."

He took a black velvet box from the plastic bag he'd set beside him on the bed, then turned to her and slid her shirt over her head until she stood naked before him, shivering with excitement and nervousness.

"This was first given to my great-grandmother."

He took a strand of shimmering pearls from the box and clasped them around her throat, letting them drop to the cleft between her breasts. She didn't need to be told they were real.

"You're more luminous than the pearls." He bent and kissed her, cupping her breasts as he moaned with pleasure.

Words weren't enough to tell him how she loved him. She reached out and touched his strong, beautiful face, then slowly unbuttoned his shirt.

His sigh sounded suspiciously like a harrumph.

"You made that sound!"

"Then you, my darling princess, must name my penalty."

"A billion trillion kisses," she said without hesitation, claiming the first with parted lips. "One for every star in the universe."

"Then I must begin now."

Hours later the bed rocked him gently to sleep, his head cradled on her shoulder, his hand resting on downy softness. Leigh lay wide-eyed, staring up at the shadowy mirror and the image of her prince.

Dear Reader,

Readers are an author's life blood and the stories couldn't happen without you. Thank you so much for reading!

If you enjoyed *Royal Groom,* Pam and I would so appreciate a review. You have no idea how much it means to us. You are the best!

If you'd like to keep up with our latest releases, you

can sign up for Lori's newsletter @ https://loriwilde.com/sign-up/.

To check out our other books, you can visit us on the web @ www.loriwilde.com.

Love and light,

Lori and Pam

# ABOUT THE AUTHORS

## Pam Andrews Hanson

Before teaming up with Lori Wilde, Pam Andrews Hanson co-wrote more than fifty novels with her mom, including romance and cozy mysteries. She is a former journalist and currently teaches freshmen composition in a university English department.

## Lori Wilde

Lori Wilde is the New York Times, USA Today and Publishers' Weekly bestselling author of 90 works of romantic fiction.

Her books have been translated into 26 languages, with more than four million copies of her books sold worldwide.

Her breakout novel, *The First Love Cookie Club*, has been optioned for a TV movie.

Lori is a registered nurse with a BSN from Texas Christian University. She holds a certificate in forensics, and is also a certified yoga instructor.

A fifth generation Texan, Lori lives with her

husband, Bill, in the Cutting Horse Capital of the World; where they run Epiphany Orchards, a writing/creativity retreat for the care and enrichment of the artistic soul.